MISTER PARADISE

AND OTHER ONE-ACT PLAYS

BY TENNESSEE WILLIAMS

PLAYS

Baby Doll & Tiger Tail
Camino Real
Candles to the Sun
Cat on a Hot Tin Roof
Clothes for a Summer Hotel
Fugitive Kind
The Glass Menagerie
A Lovely Sunday for Creve Coeur
Mister Paradise and Other One-Act Plays
Not About Nightingales
The Notebook of Trigorin
Something Cloudy, Something Clear
Spring Storm
Stairs to the Roof
Stopped Rocking and Other Screen Plays
A Streetcar Named Desire
Sweet Bird of Youth

THE THEATRE OF TENNESSEE WILLIAMS, VOLUME I
Battle of Angels, A Streetcar Named Desire, The Glass Menagerie
THE THEATRE OF TENNESSEE WILLIAMS, VOLUME II
The Eccentricities of a Nightingale, Summer and Smoke,
The Rose Tattoo, Camino Real
THE THEATRE OF TENNESSEE WILLIAMS, VOLUME III
Cat on a Hot Tin Roof, Orpheus Descending, Suddenly Last Summer
THE THEATRE OF TENNESSEE WILLIAMS, VOLUME IV
Sweet Bird of Youth, Period of Adjustment, The Night of the Iguana
THE THEATRE OF TENNESSEE WILLIAMS, VOLUME V
The Milk Train Doesn't Stop Here Anymore, Kingdom of Earth
(The Seven Descents of Myrtle), Small Craft Warnings, The Two-Character Play
THE THEATRE OF TENNESSEE WILLIAMS, VOLUME VI
27 Wagons Full of Cotton and Other Short Plays
THE THEATRE OF TENNESSEE WILLIAMS, VOLUME VII
In the Bar of a Tokyo Hotel and Other Plays
THE THEATRE OF TENNESSEE WILLIAMS, VOLUME VIII
Vieux Carré, A Lovely Sunday for Creve Coeur, Clothes for a Summer Hotel,
The Red Devil Battery Sign

27 Wagons Full of Cotton and Other Plays
The Two-Character Play
Vieux Carré

POETRY

Collected Poems
In the Winter of Cities

PROSE

Collected Stories
Hard Candy and Other Stories
One Arm and Other Stories
The Roman Spring of Mrs. Stone
The Selected Letters of Tennessee Williams, Volume I
The Selected Letters of Tennessee Williams, Volume II
Where I Live: Selected Essays

Cameron Folmar and Myk Watford in the original production of
And Tell Sad Stories of the Deaths of Queens . . .
at the Shakespeare Theatre in Washington D.C.
Photo by Richard Termine; used by permission.

MISTER PARADISE

AND OTHER ONE-ACT PLAYS BY

TENNESSEE WILLIAMS

EDITED, WITH AN INTRODUCTION AND NOTES, BY
NICHOLAS MOSCHOVAKIS
AND DAVID ROESSEL

FOREWORD BY
ELI WALLACH AND ANNE JACKSON

A NEW DIRECTIONS BOOK

Mister Paradise and Other One-Act Plays is published by special arrangement with The University of the South, Sewanee, Tennessee.

And Tell Sad Stories of the Deaths of Queens... was first published in a slightly different ver-sion in *Political Stages: Plays That Shaped A Century*, edited by Emily Mann and David Roessel; Applause Theatre & Cinema Books, 2002. *These Are the Stairs You Got to Watch* was first published in a slightly different version in a deluxe special limited edition by Librix Continuum in 2004.

Book design by Sylvia Frezzolini Severance
Manufactured in the United States of America
New Directions Books are printed on acid-free paper.
First published as New Directions Paperbook 1007 in 2005
Published simultaneously in Canada by Penguin Canada Books, Ltd.

Library of Congress Cataloging-in-Publication Data

Williams, Tennessee, 1911–1983.
  Mister Paradise and other one-act plays / by Tennessee Williams ; edited,
  with an introduction and notes, by Nicholas Moschovakis and David Roessel ;
  foreword by Eli Wallach and Anne Jackson.
    p. cm.— (New Directions paperbook ; 1007)
  Includes bibliographical references.
  ISBN 978-0-8112-1620-3 (pbk. : acid-free paper)
  I. Moschovakis, Nicholas Rand, 1969– II. Roessel, David E. (David Ernest), 1954–
  III. Title.
  PS3545.I5365M55 2005
  812'.54—dc22   2004028183
SECOND PRINTING

New Directions Books are published for James Laughlin
by New Directions Publishing Corporation
80 Eighth Avenue, New York, NY 10011

CONTENTS

FOREWORD: A TWO-HANDER

ANNE: Maureen Stapleton, one of Tennessee Williams's favorite actresses, was asked by an interviewer why she chose to perform in his plays that dealt with homosexuality, incest and cannibalism. She answered: "Well, to quote Tennessee, 'They're just folks!'"

ELI: But, we do not agree with the question posed by the interviewer who was sensationalizing and trivializing Williams's characters. Because Tennessee's "just folks" were those down on their luck, lost souls trying to make their way in a cruel world. As actors we were fortunate enough to take on the problems of those characters and bring them alive on stage. Tennessee gave them humor as well as pain, and breathed into them a nobility of spirit.

ANNE: We first met when we were cast in Tennessee's one-act play *This Property is Condemned* for Equity Library Theater. It was a two-hander. I thought Eli was too old for the part . . .

ELI: . . . because at the reading I appeared in my Captain's uniform—having just been discharged from the army—and on final leave as a Medical Administrative Officer.

ANNE: I took the director, Terry Hayden, aside and whispered "Don't you think he's too old to play the fifteen-year-old boy?" She answered, "I saw him act and we'll be lucky if he agrees to do it."

ELI: Obviously I agreed because I came to the first rehearsal dressed in knickers and a cut-up fedora covered with baseball buttons . . .

ANNE: . . . I never questioned Eli's ability to play any age or character again. I first met Tennessee when I auditioned for and was cast in his play, *Summer and Smoke*. The director came down to the footlights and said, "I'd like you to meet your author." I imagined a tall Eugene O'Neill poetic type with sunken cheeks and soulful eyes. Instead a chubby little man, beautifully groomed in a white panama suit, carrying a gold cigarette holder, came giggling down the aisle and said, "I'm happy to have you as Nelly Ewell in my new play."

ELI: My first encounter with Williams occurred when he came to the Actors Studio to watch a scene from his phantasmagoric one-act fantasy, *Ten Blocks on the Camino Real*. The director, Elia Kazan, had invited Tennessee to see a scene from the play in which I played Kilroy, an ex-boxer just discharged from the Navy. Williams almost jumped out of his seat at the end of the scene—"I'll enlarge this one-acter into a full play, and it will be done on Broadway! Can I count on you to direct it?" he asked Kazan. "We'll cross that bridge when we come to it," Kazan answered—three years later I played Kilroy in the full-length *Camino Real* on Broadway, directed by Kazan. As he left the room after seeing the scene at the Studio, Tennessee stopped at the door, stroked his chin, and said to me, "I think you'd be just right for the role of the truck driver, Mangiacavallo, in my new play, *The Rose Tattoo*. Cheryl Crawford is producing it—give her a call." And he giggled and went out the door.

ANNE: While *The Rose Tattoo* was being prepared we continued to work on Williams's one-act plays. Karl Malden directed me in *Mooney's Kid Don't Cry*, with Kevin McCarthy at the Actors Studio.

ELI: I was asked by Joshua Logan at the Actors Studio to direct *Hello From Bertha*, a play about an over-the-hill prostitute who was being evicted from her apartment. I was struck by Tennessee's empathy and sensitivity for the plight of the women—as American officers in North Africa we were ordered to raid the whorehouses to protect the health of our soldiers . . .

ANNE: After *Camino Real*, Eli was fortunate to be cast in Williams's first original film and to be directed in it by Elia Kazan. Williams had stitched together two of his one-act plays, *The Unsatisfactory Supper* and *Twenty-seven Wagons Full of Cotton*, to create the screenplay for the film he called *Baby Doll*, which also starred Karl Malden and Carol Baker.

ELI: Anne and I continued our friendship with Williams for decades and in the late 1980s we put together an evening of scenes from his plays called *Tennessee Williams Remembered*. Woven between the scenes we perform are anecdotes and memories from many pleasant evenings spent with Tennessee.

ANNE: So, you've come on a little trip through the past and our relationship with Tennessee. And now 50-some years after that trip began, a cache of Williams's earliest one-act plays has been unearthed by diligent scholars Nicholas Moschovakis and David Roessel. *Mister Paradise* is the title play of this collection. It is ironic and just, at the same time, that the theme of the play deals with the voice of a poet who is forgotten and defeated. A young woman, a poet herself, seeks him out. She's found a copy of his book of poetry being used to balance the shortened leg of an old table in an antique shop in "the Quarter." She visits Mr. Paradise with the hope of bringing his work to the attention of the public once again.

ELI: *Mister Paradise* is like an x-ray look into Williams's soul—
it is acidic, sad, and most moving. Yes. Tennessee was a
poet, and it is the poetry in his plays that gives them their
unmistakable signature. His early plays are rich with explo-
ration of different theatrical styles. Just as young painters
make their stabs at impressionism and cubism, in these one-
acts Williams tried his hand with political satire, expres-
sionism, social realism, and even drawing-room comedy,
influenced by playwrights such as Phillip Barry and S.N.
Behrman—the wife in *The Fat Man's Wife* is described by
Williams as the "Lynne Fontainne type." But the delightful
sophistication of Tennessee's wit and humor always comes
refreshingly through in his own distinctive voice. . . .

ANNE: This book is a treasure trove that actors will come to again
and again—professional, college actors, and even some
high school students. . . . These thirteen "new" one-acts,
along with the dozens of other one-acts Williams wrote,
served as inspiration and the training ground for his well-
known full-length plays.

ELI: In each of these one-acts there are elements of Williams's
courage, his sensitivity to the outsiders of life, his wicked
sense of humor, and most of all his compassion. It is a wonder to be reminded of Tennessee's gifts.

ANNE: The character of Anthony Paradise puts it this way:

> "The motion of life is upwards, the motion
> of death is down. Only the blindest of all
> blind fools can fail to see which is going to
> be finally—highest up! Not death, but life,
> my dear. Life—*life*! I defy them to stop it
> forever! Not with all their guns, not with all
> their destruction! We will keep on singing.

Someday the air all over the earth will be full
of our singing."

ELI: We wish you a happy read.

> Anne Jackson and Eli Wallach
> New York City,
> November 2004

INTRODUCTION

"THOSE RARE ELECTRICAL THINGS BETWEEN PEOPLE"

Paradise, in the mind of Tennessee Williams, could be a practically infinite number of things. It might be the world of Laura Wingfield's beautiful, transparent animals in *The Glass Menagerie* —or that of the gentlemen-callers, those temptingly human creatures who crowded sitting-rooms in her mother Amanda's youth. Paradise could be the reward, in a spiritual sense, for Alma Winemiller's moral purity during the greater part of Williams's *Summer and Smoke*. Or, is paradise instead what awaits Alma in the embrace of the stranger she meets in a public park at the play's conclusion?

To regain paradise, to retrace the road to pleasure in a world of pain and loss, is the common dream of many of Williams's characters. Twice in the present collection, we encounter young women who, having brushed against stray pieces of heaven, beat paths in its pursuit to the doors of men whom they have never met. In both plays, the men are writers—one of them an unknown, invented by Williams, and the other a real person whom he admired to the point of adulation, the eccentric prophet D. H. Lawrence. What the two women want and need differs, and the authors also receive their guests in markedly dissimilar ways. Each, though, is driven by the desire to see more of what she has glimpsed through the windows of her ordinary world, outside it and above it and beyond it—leading to a singular encounter of the kind that Lawrence defines, in Williams's lustrous phrase, as "one of those rare electrical things between people."

In *Mister Paradise and Other One-Act Plays*, the public can now read edited versions of thirteen scripts that Williams completed, but never published. Twelve are made available here for the first time, while the thirteenth—the provocative *And Tell Sad Stories of the Deaths of Queens . . .* —appears in a revised and corrected version. Among the situations and characters newly presented here, readers may discover unsuspected patches of poetic beauty and insight. At the very least, they will be rewarded for their curiosity in tracing some new pathways in the lush world of Williams's imagination.

* * *

In the title play of this volume, Paradise is a man who writes poetry. More precisely, "Anthony Paradise" is his pen name. The fact that the titular protagonist in *Mister Paradise* is actually an obscure man named Jonathan Jones, living a life of "intense disorder" somewhere in New Orleans' French Quarter, is unimportant to his existence as an author. That existence will only begin— as he informs his most ardent reader, a wealthy college girl—after "Jones has stopped breathing." In the truest sense, then, "Paradise" represents Jones's afterlife. With the belated fame won by his *nom de plume*, he hopes to find his redemption, a reward for all that he has endured as a writer, suffering like another Saint Anthony in the desert to create what his young admirer calls the "infinite wonder" of his poems.

The fashioning of a literary *persona* was almost as important to Tennessee Williams as it is to Jonathan Jones. Until the end of 1938, as a largely unknown writer, Williams published poems and stories under his given name, Thomas Lanier (or "Tom" or "T. L.") Williams. It was then that he adopted the assumed name under which he became famous. To bemused audiences in the 1940s, when he first achieved recognition, "Tennessee Williams" sounded like a hillbilly name, but to posterity it is one of the most significant names in twentieth-century literature. In recent years, like the student who tracks down Jones in "Mister Paradise," scholars have begun ringing the doorbell to the archives of Williams's unpublished manuscripts and typescripts. Much of what they have found there is both interesting in itself, and also illuminating to students and performers of his better known works.

We hope that the publication of *Mister Paradise And Other One-Act Plays* may add to the "infinite wonder" that audiences and readers around the world have felt, and continue to feel, in response to Williams's work. To the best of our knowledge, none of the plays in this volume was published or performed while Williams lived. However, in the decades since his passing in 1983, both Williams's neglected later dramas and the little-known productions of his youth have excited some attention on the stage and in print. As of March 2005, within a two year period nine of the plays included here will have received posthumous world premieres.

The texts of the thirteen plays in this book are edited versions, faithful to Williams's working drafts. For the scholar preparing a posthumous edition, true paradise would be the opportunity to ask the author's own opinion concerning every decision that affects a work's content or appearance. Unfortunately—or, perhaps, fortunately for us—we haven't yet found a way to that afterlife where Williams waits to tell us just what he thinks of our efforts. Interested readers can read a brief history of Williams's early unpublished one-acts, as well as a detailed account of our editorial policies, and of the rationale behind our most consequential choices, in our Notes on the Text.

It is safe to say that Williams wrote the majority of these plays (i.e., all except probably two of them) during the period from the mid-1930s through the late 1940s, before he achieved national recognition for *The Glass Menagerie*. In many cases, it is difficult to date his work on various drafts of a given one-act any more precisely. Clues may help us propose tentative dates for most of the plays, though such clues are often subject to interpretation. *Mister Paradise*, for instance, was almost certainly completed sometime after Williams's first trip to New Orleans at the end of 1938, though we cannot know exactly how long afterward. A very different draft that survives in the archives is set in Greenwich Village, a place where Williams first found himself in

1940, but which was notorious enough as a bohemian enclave that he need not have seen it in order to set a play in it. The New Orleans version of *Mister Paradise,* which we prefer, contains a speech that seems to anticipate or echo some lines from *The Glass Menagerie* (1944). Mr. Paradise says, "Today the world is interested in gunpowder. Poetry cannot compete with the sound of bursting shells." Both the tone and the message instantly put us in mind of Tom Wingfield's words, "All the world was waiting for bombardments!" and, "nowadays the world is lit by lightning!" And yet, we know that as early as 1937, Williams had already completed *Me, Vashya!,* a play about a munitions magnate. All that we can certainly conclude from such recurrent echoes is that, throughout the turbulent 1930s and the war years that followed, Williams's mind frequently returned to thoughts of the artist's place in a violent world.

Already as a youth, writing amid the uncertainties of the Depression and wartime America, Williams had begun to climb the heights of transcendent artistic achievement. Meanwhile, though, in day-to-day life, perhaps the closest thing to paradise that he and other Americans could ordinarily hope for was a trip to the movies. Certainly such cinematic outings provided a respite from the stifling atmosphere at home due to the suspicious, guilt-inducing vigilance of the writer's mother, Edwina Estelle Dakin Williams. In *The Glass Menagerie,* the Edwina-like Amanda Wingfield complains to to her son Tom, "I don't believe that you go every night to the movies. . . . Nobody in their right minds goes to the movies as often as you pretend to." So it is no surprise to find that Williams eventually set a short play—*These Are the Stairs You Got to Watch*—in the lobby of a movie theater, where, night after night, things go on that would have given his mother conniptions.

These Are the Stairs You Got to Watch is about a naive sixteen-year-old boy's first day working as an usher at the Joy Rio cinema. Set "in a large city on the American gulf-coast," this outrageous comedy originated, like *Mister Paradise,* sometime after

Williams first visited New Orleans in 1938. Internal evidence shows that in its present form, however, it was not completed until 1948 or after. In a letter of 1943, Williams had reported his own employment as "an usher at the Strand Theatre on Broadway, one of the swanky movie palaces," wearing "an evening uniform, midnight blue with satin lapels." Regarding the chaos that erupts in *These are the Stairs You Got to Watch*, Williams's comment in a 1943 letter to a friend that "The ushers at the Strand ought to have football uniforms with catcher's masks" is most *á propos*.

Readers of Williams's fiction will notice that this playlet has elements in common with a short story, "The Mysteries of the Joy Rio," which deals with the allure of the upper balconies of the movie house. The protagonist of "The Mysteries of the Joy Rio," a middle-aged gay man named Pablo Gonzales, finds his "earthly heaven" of anonymous sexual fulfillment in the cinema's dark and forbidden upper galleries. Similarly, *These Are the Stairs You Got to Watch* alludes to the sexuality of Mr. Kroger, who is the theater's current manager (not its former manager, the role assigned to the late "Emiel Kroger" in "The Mysteries of the Joy Rio"). In *These Are the Stairs You Got to Watch,* at least according to the boy's older co-worker Carl, Mr. Kroger initiates new hires with a (figurative) trip up the stairs. As the action chaotically escalates, Carl makes this allegation essentially a charge of sexual abuse. This insinuation raises psychological as well as ethical issues that make this play quite different from "The Mysteries of the Joy Rio," where Gonzales suffers merely for living as a "morphodite" and seeking his moments of paradise consensually in the company of strange men.

Williams's main focus in *These Are the Stairs You Got to Watch,* however, is on the shy young teenager spending his first hours on the job. The boy is a young man with little experience of sex or the world, but who has two published poems. In Williams's own poem, "The Dangerous Painters," the most charged and disturbing artwork is that which can only be found at the top of a flight of stairs:

I told him about the galleries upstairs,
the gilt and velour insulation of dangerous painters.

We feel instinctively that the poems of the young usher in *These Are the Stairs You Got To Watch* will improve, once he makes the decision to go upstairs to join a lascivious nymphet named Gladys. Flights of stairs—leading up to a celestial refuge from the worldly rat-race—are a repeated motif in Williams's early work, especially in the play *Stairs to the Roof.* However, in the Joy Rio cinema, the stairs represent not a romantic escape to a new Eden, but the knowledge of a decidedly earthly sexuality: what the young usher must climb toward is that intermittent, often transgressive corporeal enjoyment which was so central to Williams's imagination.

There are other plays here that depict themes of adolescence and age, but in terms other than those of erotic experience. *The Palooka* shares its title with a movie Williams may well have seen on its first release in 1934. We may be sure in any case that he intended an allusion to the boxing champion in Ham Fisher's popular comic strip, "Joe Palooka," which was the basis for the film and which gained a massive audience during the 1930s. Also, if Williams wrote *The Palooka* after 1937, he may have been influenced by the Clifford Odets play, *Golden Boy.* Regardless of these points of reference, Galveston Joe, the aging prizefighter in *The Palooka,* is a prototypical Williams character. He indulges himself in reveries of faded glory, and in the fabrication of happy endings for a sadly diminished life.

Galveston Joe's young interlocutor, an aspirant to fame in the ring known only as the "Kid," is as starry-eyed in his own way as the college girl in *Mister Paradise.* The Kid is all too happy to fantasize about the coming glory days that he imagines will last forever.

The comic-strip Joe Palooka was an all-American hero, one who enlisted voluntarily in the army during World War Two. Interestingly, Williams would borrow again from Fisher's strip in his longer dramatic allegory of American politics and society, *Camino Real*. Williams wrote and published an early one-act version, *Ten Blocks on the Camino Real*, soon after the war was won. The play's patriotically named protagonist, Kilroy, is a light heavyweight champion like Galveston Joe. It seems, then, that in *The Palooka* we may have one of Williams's earliest inklings of his mythic American "has-been," the fighter with a heart of gold who fights through the sixteen surrealistic "blocks"—or, rounds—of *Camino Real*. (A tempting, if unproven biographical scenario is that in the later 1940s, Williams, having previously written *The Palooka* and read or seen a performance of *Golden Boy*, alchemized his revived memories of Galveston Joe—along with some features of the hustler character, Oliver Winemiller, from Williams's postwar story "One Arm"—into the picaresque Kilroy: a postwar palooka with golden gloves.)

Another apparently early play that is also briefly, yet confidently executed, and that is quite fascinating in relation to Williams's other work, is the sketch entitled *Escape*. To a greater extent than general readers and theatergoers may realize, Williams felt a concern for the circumstances of African Americans' lives, especially in the south. In 1947, for instance, Williams published a personal apology in the *New York Times* for being unable to prevent the opening of a production of *The Glass Menagerie* at the National Theatre in Washington, D.C., where only whites were admitted. A number of Williams's writings indict southern white racism in ways that specifically reflect the plight of the Scottsboro Boys, the nine Black youths who in 1931 were falsely accused of raping two white women on a freight train near Decatur, Alabama. Williams recognized that for African American men living in such circumstances, paradise was the train that would take them to the north if they could only hop aboard. *Escape* puts such an attempt on the stage, as three convicts in a bunkhouse listen while their cellmate makes a run to the tracks for the Cannonball, with hounds and guards in full pursuit. Much later, Williams remained preoccupied with such desperate measures, and with the social and historical circumstances that made them necessary. In his brilliant play from 1957, *Orpheus Descending*, the characters Val and Vee talk about how they have witnessed "Awful! Things!" such as "Lynchings!" and "Runaway convicts torn to pieces by hounds!"

The earliest concrete date that appears, in Williams's own hand, on a text published here is February, 1935; the play is *Why Do You Smoke So Much, Lily?* Here the twenty-three-year-old playwright introduced a conflict that would reappear in many of his other works: the struggle between a psychologically frustrated adolescent and his or her parents. A good example is the one-act play, *Auto-da-Fé*, in which a young man's sexuality is repressed by a rigidly moralistic mother reminiscent, as usual, of Edwina. In *Why Do You Smoke So Much, Lily?*, however, the subject is that of a lonely woman troubled by mental instability or illness, a figure which recurs often in Williams's later one-acts. After creating the character of Lily, he went on to write a number of other short plays featuring other avatars of Shakespeare's Ophelia. These include *The Lady of Larkspur Lotion, Portrait of a Madonna*, and Williams's last one-act play, the posthumously published and performed *The One Exception*.

Why Do You Smoke So Much, Lily? carries the subtitle, "A Short Story in One Act." In fact, Williams adapted this script directly from an unpublished story, which is filed together with the dramatic version in the Ransom Center archives. The scene is set in "a fashionable apartment in the west end of Saint Louis," where Williams's own family lived at that time. We cannot doubt that the character of the nervous, traumatized Lily was modelled on Williams's older sister Rose—who also smoked, and suffered from "nerves" and sexual frustration—and the character of Mrs. Yorke on their mother. However, such obvious parallels always tell only a small part of the story. Lily, like her late father, but unlike Williams's father Cornelius, is "the intellectual type." Even more curiously, Lily's "features are biggish. . . . She would make a rather good-looking young man." Is Lily Yorke drawn, in part, from Williams's piteous view of his own situation at twenty-three? In early 1935, living at home, Williams must have felt only slightly less confined and frustrated than his sister, or Lily in the play. No doubt Williams, too, fantasized about escaping through what Mrs. Yorke calls the "filthy fiction" that was written by "Bohemians, Bolsheviks," and published in "trashy, new-fangled magazines." When he was not reading such stuff, he was doing his best to write it himself.

Escape is the central theme in another, comparable play, *Summer at the Lake*, about the sixteen-year-old Donald Fenway and his mother; in fact, a draft of this play bears the title "Escape" (see Notes on the Text). The play could have been inspired by *The Sea Gull* of Williams's beloved Chekhov, whose character Madame Arkadina complains: "Tell me, what's wrong with my son? Why is he so depressed and ill-humoured? He spends whole days on the lake and I hardly ever see him." In *Summer at the Lake*, Donald desperately seeks a place of refuge from Mrs. Fenway's harried sensibility, and from her perpetual nagging on topics that seem alternately trivial and all too painfully pertinent to his future. Like Tom Wingfield in *The Glass Menagerie*, Donald is denounced by his mother as a "dreamer" without a future, and (in her judgment) justifies her disappointment in him by fleeing the house as often as he can to pursue his only pleasure, swimming on the lake, where "time" is suspended, and a dreamer can go "floating off into space" without restriction.

Williams, himself, was a regular swimmer; but this is not the only characteristic that he shared with Donald Fenway. At one point in *Summer at the Lake*, Mrs. Fenway asks her son whether he has "fallen in love;" he answers "No." She replies, "I wish you had. Then there might be some excuse for your acting so queerly." Later, Mrs. Fenway for the second time voices a fear that Donald has begun to to seem "different—or queer or something," and that others will start calling Donald "not like the other boys." Here, presented in the only terms that Williams probably considered acceptable to potential audiences when he wrote this play, we are granted a glimpse into one of many possible motives for Donald's need to escape his identity, as dictated by his family and the world he knows. At the same time, it is significant that young Donald seems considerably worse off than Tom Wingfield, Lily Yorke, or Tom Williams, since Donald lacks any intellectual or creative outlet.

When Williams was Donald's age (many years before he created the character), he could at least be assured that his mother had a high opinion of his "talent," for Edwina doted on her son even as she oppressed him. Nonetheless, the impatient apprehensions of futility felt by the adolescent who lacks conventional aspirations for adulthood, or even any sense of what a happy adulthood might amount to, were not too distant from Williams's own feelings during the 1930s when he wrote this play. The Fenways' cottage probably recalls a visit that Williams made in 1933 to Lake Taneycomo, in the Ozark Mountains, together with his mother and his younger brother. By the summer of 1933, Williams was already twenty-two, but he was still far away from obtaining a college degree or finding a vocation that would make him financially independent. Instead he was being bored by his work at the International Shoe Company, where his father had connections, and chafing under the regime of life in the family's Saint Louis home. At the end of *Summer at the Lake*, Williams allows the audience to decide whether Donald finally escapes his predicament and, if so, how.

Williams spent more time redrafting and revising *Summer at the Lake* than most of the other plays published here, if we may judge by the amount of material that has survived in the archives. He must have produced the latest complete drafts, including our copy-text, during the late 1930s (but before 1939). A few years earlier, probably between 1935 and 1937, he had written *The Big Game*, another drama about young manhood in America. Set in a hospital ward, in a city that can be identified as Saint Louis, the play sets the pathos of a terminally ill youth, Dave, and the terrifying brain cancer of an older man, Walton, against the vitality of a celebrated college halfback named Tony Elson. The playing injury that has taken Tony off the field and into the ward is, to him, only a minor nuisance. He is far more alive, physically, than the other two men put together. Moreover, he constantly attracts the sexual attention that, to Dave, can be nothing more than a hopeless dream of paradise. Yet it is only after Tony's release from the hospital, and his disappearance from the stage, that Dave and Walton begin their electrical exchange on death and eternity, which gives this play its distinction. Walton, a veteran of the trenches of World War I, introduces Dave to the contemplation of the eternity: "Know what I did last night? I got up and raised the window shade! I raised it as high as it would go! . . . So that I could look at the stars!" At the play's conclusion, we watch Dave do the same.

In his *Memoirs* of 1975, Williams gave an account of how he went to New York in the fall of 1939 to meet his agent Audrey Wood. "I had not rested or shaved, and looked pretty disreputable when I presented myself at the imposing offices of Liebling-Wood, Inc. . . . she said, 'Well, well, you've finally made it,' to which I replied, 'Not yet.' I meant this not as a witticism but quite literally." Probably about one year earlier than this episode (as he remembered it in the *Memoirs*), Williams had written *The Fat Man's Wife*, in which an influential producer, Joe Cartwright, tells his wife Vera: "You could have knocked me over with a feather when that big hillbilly Merriwether walked into my office the first time. Here I was expecting an extremely polished, high-brow, cosmopolitan sort of person . . . and in walks a guy who looks like he just stepped out of a back-home cartoon!"

The introduction of a playwright, one with a hillbilly image, to New York theatrical circles was not Williams's only prescient conception in *The Fat Man's Wife*. Cartwright has also been complaining about how the writer, Dennis Merriwether, resists commercial alterations to his dramatic work, crying that "the artist in him" would be crucified. A cliché premise, no doubt—but one that uncannily foreshadows Williams's own experience in 1944 with Louis Singer, *The Glass Menagerie*'s original producer, who urged Williams to give the play a happy ending.

In *The Fat Man's Wife*, Dennis plans to leave New York for Acapulco rather than compromise his art. He is not, however, above trying to reshape his own story happily. But when he tries to induce Vera Cartwright to abscond with him, she declines. The scenario seems to owe at least a glancing debt to Bernard Shaw's *Candida*, in which another married woman rejects the offers of a passionate young poet. In 1940, when Williams himself travelled from New York to Acapulco, it was to escape the memory of rejection by his first great love, Kip Kiernan, who felt unable to grant Williams's request that he stay with him and—as Dennis puts it—to "steer by the stars" beside him.

Ten years later, a more outwardly satisfied Williams would write to Elia Kazan, "I don't write with the effervescence that I used to. It comes harder. The peak of my virtuosity was in the one-act plays, some of which are like fire-crackers in a rope. Some of that came from sexual repression and loneliness which don't exist anymore for very good reasons, and some of it came from plain youth and freshness." Here Williams was not fairly judging the quality of the writing in his mature full-length plays, yet there was, certainly, a spontaneity to the short form that he might well have missed in 1950. One of the more playful one-offs that resulted from his earlier, whimsical sense of freedom was *The Pink Bedroom*, which adapts elements of a story that Williams had entered in a university fiction contest under the same title in 1931.

Though there were some parts of the concept for *The Pink Bedroom* that originated very early, it is also interesting to note that Williams listed the title among other completed scripts ready for publication twelve years later, in the spring of 1943. This listing indicates that he probably produced the present version then, or slightly earlier (see our Notes on the Text). In *The Pink Bedroom*, the Woman's sentimental attachment to a plainly tedious and negligent lover—whom she has, in fact, already replaced—is farcical, if not necessarily the tactic of a juvenile dramatist. The play's effect hinges on this mild absurdity in its resolution, but also on Williams's experiments in disjointed dialogue.

Whereas the estranged couple's mutual interruptions and explosive ejaculations may seem merely to travesty those of Othello or of operatic protagonists, they may also look vaguely ahead, in the long trajectory of Williams's career, to the impulse that finally breaks dialogue down into fragments (in texts such as *In the Bar of a Tokyo Hotel*). As employed here, however, to merely comic purposes, the style is one that doesn't typify Williams's work at any age.

Of all the plays in this book, *Thank You, Kind Spirit* is the one that we are able to date with the greatest precision. Williams wrote it in New Orleans on or before Tuesday, October 21, 1941: most likely that very morning, or on the previous day, and certainly within the week or two weeks preceding that date (see our Note on the play). The play's central figure is an old octoroon woman who converses with spirits. Like Billy in *Escape*, this African American character is also assaulted, in this case by a crowd incited by a woman and her Catholic priest. The crowd eventually dismantles the woman's place of business, but the language suggests that this is another sort of lynching. "Yes, nigger—nigger! Call yourself Creole, dontcha?—That's just one of her lies! . . . Just an ole Voodoo nigger puttin' on make-believe spirits an' in the name of Jesus, too!" Alternatively, the old spiritualist is another incarnation of the artist, who, like Tom at the opening of *The Glass Menagerie*, can say "Yes, I have tricks in my pocket, I have things up my sleeve." Her effort to to "give . . . truth in the pleasant disguise of illusion" (as Tom also said) is dismissed by the angry voice from the rear. But there is solace in the end, for true redemption begins with an audience who believes—even if it consists of just one little girl.

Williams always exalted the individual voice, as opposed to that of the crowd or its typical member. In an age of socialism and fascism, communism and anti-communism, such an uncompromising commitment to the soul's singularity was not to be taken for granted. One of Williams's eeriest, most evocative and troubling poems, "The Death Embrace," depicts a group of indistinguishable men, "mechanical, mindless puppets," who operate machines that are designed to destroy them:

> *The foreman advanced, with gas mask over his face,*
> *To read an announcement.*
> These men, *he said*, have liquidated themselves
> for the good of the State!
> *Oh, then, what applause, what a ringing of bells was started!*

Williams addresses the same twentieth-century nightmare here, in *The Municipal Abattoir*. The play's setting in a Spanish-speaking dictatorship may suggest more particular historical associations, if not a specific date of composition. Williams wrote "The Death Embrace" in Acapulco in September, 1940; and in a letter written around the same time, he asked a friend, "So the world is now swinging towards fascism—What can we do about it? What will we?" Later, when Williams wrote *The Night of the Iguana,* he would set its action in Mexico during the same period, signalling the importance of this choice by introducing a group of grotesquely nationalistic German tourists. On the other hand, *The Municipal Abattoir* also puts one in mind of Cuba, which Williams visited during the 1950s both before and after Fidel Castro's ascendancy. As in *Camino Real,* Williams voiced his skepticism of various sorts of political authority in *The Municipal Abattoir* through the paper-thin veil of a Spanish-language setting.

It is interesting to consider the premise of *The Municipal Abattoir* against Williams's other work in this collection and elsewhere. One often thinks of the iconic "Williams character" as a non-conformist trying to break away from his or her situation. In this one-act, though, the central character feels an inexorable compulsion to remain a dutiful cog in the wheel. That Williams had an ongoing interest in this side of the psychological equation is suggested in a letter of April 1947, in which he stated that he had developed a "passion for Kafka."

D. H. Lawrence, one of the greatest of modern individualists, had an earlier and more profound influence on Williams' thought and writing. In July, 1939, Williams hitchhiked north from Southern California to San Francisco. He then happened to be reading from a book of Lawrence's letters, which he had borrowed from a public library—as ever, seeking a deeper insight into the lives of those authors whose work he found most compelling. He felt that he had found a kindred spirit in Lawrence, as he himself put it: "[I] feel so much understanding & sympathy for him—though his brilliance makes me feel very humble & inadequate." Inadequate, that is, to the task of writing a play about Lawrence, which Williams tried on several occasions to do. During the 1940s he worked on a number of projects relating to the writer's life, including a dramatization of the story "You Touched Me," co-authored with Donald Windham; a one-act titled *The Case of the Crushed Petunias* that drew partly on the story "The Fox"; and a contemplated full-length play based on Lawrence's life, later reduced to the form of a one-act and published as *I Rise in Flame, Cried the Phoenix*. Yet another, contrasting expression of Williams's awe for Lawrence's powers appears here, in the play *Adam and Eve on a Ferry*.

With its references to the ride across San Francisco Bay, *Adam and Eve on a Ferry* was most likely inspired by Williams's journey through Lawrence's letters on the trip to California mentioned above. Therefore, he may well have written the one-act in late 1939 or early 1940, though a slightly later date is also plausible. In May, 1942, after completing a draft of *You Touched Me!*, Williams typed a page of prefatory notes to this full-length comedy. His comments stressed "the message of Lawrence: his praise of life and abhorrence of the negative . . . his insistence on the hot, quick, direct <u>vital</u> contact between people as opposed to the deadness of polite social relations. His belief in the almost mystic importance of physical communion. His hatred of shut-in places and people and his belief in the dynamic acceptance of life—Going out, not in. His opposition to sterile intellectualism. Love of honesty, his pure, light, fearless attitude toward reality. The power of the unconscious fighting its way through restrictions, taboos. The life force." At the same time, Williams wrote concerning the script that he and Windham had just written: "In the comic effects of the play there is a rather dangerous departure from what is Lawrence, for Lawrence did not have humor in the popular sense. We have put it in, frankly, to make the play more generally acceptable." Elsewhere, however, Williams described his sense of Lawrence as "a funny little man."

These varied remarks provide an interesting context for Williams's conception, in *Adam and Eve on a Ferry,* of a fundamentally comic Lawrence: one who functions as an analyst for repressed women. This shamanistic, benignly sarcastic character is quite an entertaining figure on stage. Still, the play's sense of absurdity need not detract from what Williams may have been trying to say about the artist's more seriously therapeutic role, and the author's vision of Lawrence as an artist with a mysterious power over others' physical and psychic lives.

Paradise in Williams's world is elusive, but the impulse to remake it is creative, and people have their ways—especially when it comes to love and sex. Just off stage, in *The Glass Menagerie,* is the "Paradise Dance Hall": a place where couples meet in the evenings before disappearing, discreetly, into the shadows of the adjoining alley. In the last, longest play in the present volume, Williams draws on his own experience of a shadow world of unsanctioned sexuality. In some ways, that experience informs his writing more literally and explicitly here than in any of his other works for the stage.

And Tell Sad Stories of the Deaths of Queens . . . concerns the private life of "Candy" Delaney, a successful New Orleans interior decorator and landlord who is also a transvestite. A "play in two scenes," it was probably begun in 1957; it was then misplaced, apparently, until Williams completed it sometime near the end of the 1960s. In a letter of 1946, Williams had referred to homosexuality in America as a subject "that you can't put on the stage as it now exists." During the 1950s, the lives of "queens" and "queers" were, if anything, even harder to treat sympathetically in a public medium than they had been before the country's descent into the paranoid intolerance of Cold War culture. Even so, in 1953, Williams managed to write a minor gay character for the stage, the Baron Charlus in the non-naturalistic fantasy *Camino Real* (which met with a poor critical reception). By the end of the 1960s, a decade distinguished by its increasing frankness about sex, theatrical audiences had started to develop a more open attitude. In the early seventies, Williams even became a target of criticism for his alleged failure to champion gay liberation. In 1975 he would answer these attacks, impudently and controversially, with the scandalously flamboyant revelations of his *Memoirs*.

In a televised interview of 1971, Williams spoke proudly of the character that he had finally created in Candy Delaney: "If I wanna write a drag queen, I'll write a drag queen, and I *have* written [a play about] one, as a matter of fact, which *will* be produced someday." What originally brought Candy "out" and to New Orleans, at a time when "she" was still a teenager, was a seventeen-year relationship with an older man, a union that Williams clearly invites us to regard—legalities aside—as a marriage. Now, nearly thirty-five years old and recently abandoned for a younger rival, Candy is devastated. A photograph of her former "husband" is still exhibited, all too conspicuously, in her exquisitely decorated apartment. In spite of that lingering emotional presence, the woman in Candy's closet is about to risk exposing herself once more, "in drag" and in all the vulnerability of a heartfelt passion, and to the most unlikely of lovers. Karl is a sailor, encountered in a bar. He insists, "I don't go with queers," until Candy's money softens his resistance. For Candy, who, until the end of the play, has not yet experienced the dangers of rough trade, the play is scarcely a tragedy; Williams called it "quite funny."

From the author's journals and *Memoirs,* we know that Williams himself had suffered bodily violence on at least two occasions in 1943, at the hands of men whom he had picked up casually while cruising. The first time, he wrote angrily but philosophically, "Why do they strike us? What is our offense? We offer them a truth which they cannot bear to confess except in privacy and in the dark—a truth which is inherently as bright as the morning sun." The second time Williams recorded an incident of physical assault in his youth, his attackers were like Karl, sailors. However, it would be a mistake to regard Candy's bitter lesson as autobiographical. Rather than any sort of personal confession, *And Tell Sad Stories of the Deaths of Queens . . .* should be seen as Williams's answer to the oppressive conventions then governing ideas about homosexuality in postwar drama, film, and popular fiction, rules which dictated that gay characters must be "cured" of their sexuality or else suffer a terrible punishment, usually death, for their transgressions.

Partly because of his own homosexuality, though by no means entirely because of it, Williams had a keen eye for the ways in which violent men like Karl implicated the hypocrisy and brutality of the ruling powers of 1950s America. And yet, Williams envisioned Karl with about as much sympathy as many of the other young hustlers and petty criminals who appear throughout his drama, fiction, and verse. Karl himself is a desperate, socially and economically handicapped character whose fundamental misery blinds him to the darkness of his actions, and perhaps even to his own ultimate motives.

Williams's manuscripts show that when he began writing *And Tell Sad Stories of the Deaths of Queens . . .* , he was also experimenting with other fictional and dramatic variants. Instead of a transvestite male, some of these drafts feature an older widow or divorcée in the role of *inamorata*, while the younger object of her desire is, as here, a man. It would be difficult to say whether these alternative, heterosexual scenarios came to Williams's mind before or after the concept for the present version, with its setting in the gay subculture of the French Quarter.

What is certain is that, if Williams had completed *And Tell*

Sad Stories of the Deaths of Queens . . . in 1957 as it now exists, or even in a considerably more polished form, producers would not have given him the chance to see it performed before a mainstream audience. Moreover, its presentation would have constituted an almost unthinkable personal confession of Williams's membership in a world of covert relationships and sexual intimacy.

Williams's paradises are sometimes real, sometimes false; sometimes visible and sometimes hidden from view; at times physical, at times intangible. Always they are paradoxical. Paradise exists for us, and it cannot exist for us; it both is, and is not to be found on earth. The title of *And Tell Sad Stories of the Deaths of Queens* . . . is a tip of the hat to Shakespeare: in *Richard II,* a young king falls from the paradise of his irresponsible, self-indulgent fancies to an adult consciousness of error, folly, and mortality. Disappointed with himself and the unforgiving world, he cries:

> *For God's sake, let us sit upon the ground*
> *And tell sad stories of the death of kings.*

Williams's play parodies Richard's fall to earth, as Candy discovers the limits of love's ability to reshape the world into a remembered or imaginary paradise. Still, the play leaves Candy her friends, her material comforts and aesthetic consolations, and even her dignity. Unlike Shakespeare's king, Williams's queen proves able to laugh at her humiliations.

Nicholas Moschovakis
David Roessel
January 2005

ACKNOWLEDGMENTS

This volume would never have existed if the editors had not received joint fellowships, in the summer of 2000, from the Harry Ransom Humanities Research Center at the University of Texas at Austin. To the staff of the Ransom Center, especially Pat Fox, Tara Wenger, and Rich Oram, we are grateful for friendship and for much assistance navigating and photocopying folders in the Williams Collection. Thanks also to the Department of Special Collections at the University Research Library at the University of California, Los Angeles, and to Michael Kahn, for making their scripts available to us.

We are indebted to New Directions, in particular president Peggy Fox, for entrusting us initially with the volume of Williams's *Collected Poems* and now with this book. Were it not for Thomas Keith, our editor at New Directions, we could not have completed this edition; to him we owe many corrections and useful suggestions, as well as much fine, friendly, and consummately well-informed conversation. Jack Barbera, Robert Bray, George Crandell, Al Devlin, Philip Kolin, Colby Kullman, Brenda Murphy, Michael Paller, Barton Palmer, Brian Parker, Annette Saddik, Nancy Tischler, and others in the wonderfully supportive community of Williams scholars have shared their copious knowledge with us, formally and informally, over the past several years. Michael Paller kindly shared with us the manuscript of his forthcoming monograph on Williams and sexuality, and we have saved some face here due to his and Annette Saddik's timely corrections of our research. To Nancy Tischler and Al Devlin we are especially grateful for their ongoing volumes of the *Selected Letters;* their work has been nearly as important to us as that of the late Lyle Leverich, whose biography of Williams as a young man, *Tom: The Unknown Tennessee Williams,* will remain indispensable to scholars and critics for the foreseeable future.

For their assistance in Williams-related matters great and small, we must thank Michael Kahn, Lee Hoiby, and Jeremy Lawrence; Michael Wilson and Chris Baker of the Hartford Stage Company; Steven Mazzola, PJ Papparelli, Jef Hall-Flavin, and Liza Holtmeyer of the Shakespeare Theatre; Elizabeth Barron, Paul J. Willis, and Arin Black of the Tennessee Williams/New Orleans Literary Festival; Michael Bush and Lisa Dozier of the Manhattan Theatre Club; and, on a more personal note, David and Lu Ann Landon, Arnold Rampersad, Mike Keeley, Christine P. Horn, and Francesca McCaffery. To Pamela Beatrice, Joan and Yiannis Moschovakis, and Anna Moschovakis, much love and gratitude are due.

Above all, nearly everything that we have done as we ought in this volume owes something to Allean Hale—to her expertise, to her keen eye and memory, to her unrivalled knowledge of Williams, and to her kind generosity with her time. Needless to say, all that which we may have done badly is to be laid to our charge alone.

MISTER PARADISE

AND OTHER ONE-ACT PLAYS

THESE ARE THE STAIRS
YOU GOT TO WATCH

These Are The Stairs You Got to Watch was first performed by the Shakespeare Theatre on April 22, 2004 at the Kennedy Center in Washington D.C. It was directed by Michael Kahn; the set design was by Andrew Jackness; the costume design was by Catherine Zuber; the lighting design was by Howell Binkley; the sound design was by Martin Desjardins; and original music was composed by Adam Wernick. The cast, in order of appearance, was as follows*:

CARL, a cinema usher	Thomas Jay Ryan
BOY, a newly hired usher	Hunter Gilmore
GLADYS, a girl	Carrie Specksgoor
MAN, an older patron	Brian McMonagle
GIRL, a friend of Gladys	Janet Patton
MR. KROGER, the cinema manager	John Joseph Gallagher
CASHIER	Joan van Ark
A POLICEMAN	Myk Watford

The play can be performed with up to three policemen.

Scene: The entrance of the Joy Rio, a third-rate cinema which used to be a great old opera-house in a large city on the American gulf-coast. In another year or two the authorities will condemn the building as a public hazard and it will be demolished or perhaps it will be restored as a landmark; now forgotten and neglected, its historic glories are suggested dimly by greasy red damask, torn and blackening, and by the gilt baroque of the nymph which wantons over the bottom steps of the great marble stairs. The set will barely suggest these items, for the lighted area is very small. It includes the nymph, the bottom steps of the marble staircase and the entrance to a room marked "ladies"—and of course a door to the exterior where the ticket-box stands.

Faintly from time to time we hear the soundtrack of the film being shown. When a patron enters, his grotesquely elongated shadow is cast before him on the ancient carpet for the daylight outside is fiercely blazing.

As the curtain rises a new young usher, a schoolboy of sixteen taking summer employment, is being shown the ropes by a veteran employee of the establishment, a man of thirty named Carl. The new boy wears a dirty white mess-jacket and close-fitting sky-blue pants and he is perspiring more with nervousness than with the stifling heat of the August afternoon.

CARL [*lazily flashing his light on the roped-off staircase*]: These are the stairs you got to watch.

BOY: What for?

CARL: This here's an old opera-house. Y'know that, don't you? Them stairs go up to three galleries. I don't know, maybe four. I never counted 'em. A breeze would knock them over, and the top boxes, rows of boxes, all the way around from the right-hand side of the stage to the left-hand side of the stage. I went up to them once, only once, the day I started work here. The old guy shown me like I am showing you, only in them days it wasn't forbidden to go up them there steps which now it is, which is something you got to remember. Because if anybody slips by you and goes up there, not only do you lose your job here, that is, if Kroger finds out, but if anything happens up there in that rutten mess, which is all fallin' t'pieces, they hold you responsible for it and— What's a matter, Gladys?

[*This abrupt question is directed to a young girl, Gladys, who has entered the theatre and is loitering about the foot of the staircase.*]

GLADYS [*coldly*]: I'm waitin' fo' my girl-friend, if it's any bus'-ness of yours.

CARL: It's my bus'ness, all right, if you start messin' around in here anymore.

GLADYS: Look who's talking. Why don't you get a grown-up man's job, honey.

CARL [*flashing lamp on her precocious figure*]: Look. Did you come in here to see the show? If so get back to your seat. If not, go home, or operate on the street or at the drug-store.

GLADYS: I hate you.

CARL: That makes me suffer.

GLADYS: I bet. I bet you suffer. You suffer like a fish, you fish, you fink, you fish-faced fish of a fink! If my girl-friend comes in, little boy, I'm sittin' in the first three rows, she'll fin' me...

[*This last is addressed haughtily to the new usher as Gladys swishes out of the lighted area into the orchestra aisle. A door*] *swings open on the screen dialogue which comes up clearly for a few phrases.*]

FILM DIALOGUE: *Get up off the bed.*
                 —I'm sick!
                 —I said, Get up.

[*A slap and a scream are heard. The new usher jumps a little. Carl laughs tiredly and hikes at the waist of his trousers. The door swings shut again and the sound track fades into incoherent murmurs.*]

CARL: That Joan Bennett is a damn fine little actress, and did you know that she's a grandmother? I should have a grandmother like that. Everybody should have a grandmother like that. You seen this picture before?

[*New boy shakes his head staring big-eyed at the screen visible to him through oval glass of door.*]

CARL: There is a scene in this picture where Joan Bennett is eating a piece of celery which I want you to look at and tell me what you think. [*Suddenly.*] Hey! [*His pocket lamp stabs at a male figure slipping under the velvet rope of the staircase.*] Where do you think you're going?

MAN: I'm looking for the Gents' Room.

CARL: You know it ain't up there.

MAN: Why don't they keep this place lighted so you can see where you're going. [*He walks off.*]

CARL: You see what I mean about that old staircase? You got to watch that staircase like a hawk, 'specially this time of the day.

BOY: Yeah?

CARL [*standing close in front of him*]: How old are you?

BOY: S-seventeen!

CARL: You ain't seventeen. You ain't even used a razor yet.

[*Touches his chin.*]

BOY: The paper said "Boy seventeen or over that could work afternoons."

CARL: You're about fifteen, ain't you? Who did you talk to? Kroger? Did old man Kroger hire you? Yeh. I bet it was him, that old man's dirty, he's fruit. You know about fruit?

BOY: Fruit?

CARL: I don't mean apples and peaches. Look. Look. You don't need a job this bad that you got to work here. This here is a dirty place that's run by a dirty man and I don't even like to tell you about the sort of stuff that goes on in this place that I got to tell you if you are going to work here. Don't work here. Get you an outdoor job or a job in a drug store. I'd tell your mother if I was acquainted with her, or your old man, because I'm a parent myself. That's why I'm quitting. I been in a rut here, and it's a disgrace of a job for a grown-up man to be a rutten usher in a movie. I'm twenty-eight and I been here ten years and I'm making ten dollars more than I made when I started and now I got a wife and a three-months-old baby and the priest tells my wife that trying not to have babies is a sin. [*This is all said in a voice so enormously tired, that the words barely seem to have the strength to crawl out of the sagging lips.*] This is the restaurant scene I told you about. Look. [*He advances and pulls the swinging door to the orchestra partly open.*]

FILM DIALOGUE: —*Hors d'oeuvres, darling?*
—*No, thank you.*
—*Have a piece of celery. It's full of Vitamin B,*
which is good for the nerves.

CARL: There now! Look at that close-up!

BOY: I don't see . . .

CARL: Look, look. Look at that, will yuh.

[*An adolescent girl has entered with a greasy bag of popcorn. She stares at the two figures by the swinging doors for a moment. Then quickly steps out of her slippers and flies like a shadow up the marble staircase with the shoes in one hand. Carl turns lazily around.*]

CARL: Was that somebody?

BOY: What?

CARL: Somebody come in, didn't they?

BOY: I d-didn't see.

CARL: How did that popcorn git there?

[*Flashes pocket lamp on spilled popcorn at the base of the staircase.*]

CARL: There wasn't no popcorn there a moment ago. Somebody did come in. Look. There's popcorn on the stairs! [*Calls up.*] Hey! Hey, up there!

[*The manager Kroger enters from outside. He is a man of enormous corpulence with a quality of decay as palpable as the old building itself.*]

KROGER: What's the trouble? Did somebody get up the stairs?

CARL: Naw, sir.

KROGER: Then why are you shouting up there? What do you think I pay you guys to do, to look at the pitcher? Is that what you think you been employed to do? Two of you here, both enjoyin' the movie while anybody that wants to slips under the rope and gives the place a bad name? You boy, you new boy. What did I say to you about them stairs? Didn't I tell you you got to watch them stairs.

CARL [*sullenly*]: Nobody went up them stairs, Mr. Kroger, while I been here.

KROGER [*to the boy*]: You see anybody slip under that there rope?

BOY: —N-no, Sir . . .

CARL: All I seen was some popcorn spilt on the steps.

KROGER: Sherlock Holmes, huh? Are you sure Mr. Sherlock Holmes? If there's popcorn on them steps it didn't grow there, did it?

CARL: I'm not responsible for what's on the steps in a dirty old place like this. If the management ain't clean enough to see that the place is run decent I don't give a goddam what's on the dirty old steps, ice cream or bananas, far as I am concerned. I seen popcorn on the steps. That's all I seen.

KROGER: And you was shouting at popcorn? You think popcorn can holler? Boy! How did that stuff get there?

CARL: He don't know how it got there anymore than I do. Look, Mr. Kroger.

KROGER: Don't say 'Look' to me, boy. Don't say 'Look' to me ever.

CARL: I'll say 'Look' to you or anybody else that I want to.

KROGER: What the goddam hell do you think you're doing, talking to me that way in my own theatre?

CARL: Your own theatre, you fat old bug of a bunny, and strap it up twice for good measure. I quit. I quit this morning, have you forgotten? After ten years in the stink and sweat of this hole, I give you my notice because I come here clean and I'm going out dirty. Not my dirt but the dirt of this filthy place here, and if I talked— If I talked, Mr. Kroger! —Y'know what I could get done to this place? I could get it shut up like the blade of a knife! That quick and that easy if I just opened my mouth about half I know about what this — !

KROGER [to the boy]: Boy! Boy, step outside and call an officer here!

CARL: Yeh, yeh, do that, do that, do that, I wish you'd do that!

KROGER: I will not tolerate impertinence like that from a moron!

CARL: Why, you fat old morphodite, you! [He rips off his fancy mess jacket and throws it violently into Mr. Kroger's face.] Did you hear what I said? Morphodite? Morphodite? Old fat stinkin' old Morphodite?

[One or two patrons are attracted by the disturbance into a

9

lighted area. An excited, skinny little woman of fifty, a cashier, darts in the door.]

CASHIER: Mr. Kroger, Mr. Kroger, what is it? Were you attacking Mr. Kroger?

[*This is spoken to the boy who shakes his head in a panic.*]

CARL: *I* was attackin' Mr. Kroger, *I* was, Me, *me!* I sweated an' stunk in here in this swill a dirt an' corruption for ten long terrible years of my young life! And now I'm gonna go home an' wash the dirt off me! You hear me? Wash the dirt off me, and I ain't forgot what happened here ten years ago when I got the dirty job neither! Have you forgotten what happened here ten years ago when I got the dirty job, Kroger?

[*Kroger falls back speechless toward the outside door.*]

CASHIER: How dare you talk to Mr. Kroger like that, Carl! I don't see how you dare to talk to Mr. Kroger like that, after all he's put up with you, with you coming here drunk, with you letting girls upstairs and men after them up there like goats while you're on duty, I swear to goodness, I don't understand how you could have the nerve to open your mouth to poor old Mr. Kroger. And make this disturbance like this. You boys go back to your seats, there's nothing to look at, go on back to the picture, you boys, there.

[*The boys return into orchestra aisle. Mr. Kroger has retreated outside but his great, outraged voice can be heard summoning the law.*]

CARL: I hope he does call the law, I just hope he does call the law in this sweatin' stink-hole. If there was a cop out there he wouldn't holler. You can be goddam sure if there was a cop on that corner he wouldn't open his button loud as a whisper. [*Tears off the cummerbund and the false front shirt and the elastic black tie and throws them in a heap on the floor and kicks them.*]

CASHIER [*sobbing*]: I have never seen anybody act like this before in my life, Carl Meagre, and I have never heard language like that anywhere before in my life, and if you dare to open your mouth like that about Mr. Kroger who is sick with cancer, and you know it, why, I'm going to open my mouth about things I know concerning you and your conduct with certain girls that come here.

CARL: Go on, you prune. Take that rag-heap an' burn it. Burn it, the whole bunch of it. I came here clean and I am going out dirty, after ten years of it!

[*Carl rips down the front of the dirty sky-blue pants and kicks them off and stands before the woman in his underwear. Cashier screams and runs out into the blaze of sunlight. He kicks the sky blue pants, jerks down the velvet rope and goes upstairs to the usher's locker room. After a moment the boy slips the velvet rope back in place. After another moment or two a police car is heard drawing up to the curb outside. At the same time Gladys comes out of the orchestra section and stares curiously and provocatively at the boy who reddens and turns the front of his body away from her gaze.*]

GLADYS: Did you see my girlfriend.

[*This has no question mark. The words are said as if they had no meaning.*]

BOY: No.

GLADYS: She didn't come in. She has on a white silk blouse and big gold earrings. She went out to get some popcorn and she didn't come back.

BOY: No.

GLADYS: My girl friend is boy crazy.

[*The boy shakes his head jerkily. His hand moves jerkily from his side to his pocket and then quickly back out of his pocket again.*]

GLADYS: She's fourteen. I think it's bad to be boy crazy that young. How old are you?

BOY: —S-sixteen!

GLADYS: We are just the same age but you are blond and I'm dark. Opposite types! —I get so bored with that picture. Joan Bennett. You look at it?

BOY: No. No, I work here.

[*Gladys laughs with an air of idiotic fatigue. Woman rushes excitedly in.*]

CASHIER: Mr. Kroger, Mr. Kroger, Mr. Kroger!

GLADYS: —What?

CASHIER [*to the boy*]: Where is Mr. Kroger, in his office?

BOY: —I—I don't know!

CASHIER: Watch here! Smoke is coming out of an upstairs window!

[*She rushes back out crying for Mr. Kroger.*]

GLADYS: I know something about that woman that I wouldn't like to say, but she has got the nerve to tell me not to come to this movie because I'm too young. Do you know about this place? Kids can have lots of fun here, but they got to be careful. You have got to be careful. But if you are quick—and careful—you can have lots of fun here. You sure can have fun here if you know how to have it.

[Swinging doors open. Movie soundtrack and actress's voice are heard.]

FILM DIALOGUE: —You were gone such a long, long time and I was so lonely I really didn't want to. But I was helpless. It was stronger than I was. It was stronger than he was. Neither of us wanted it to happen, but it happened. Sometimes things just happen. Do you know what I mean?

GLADYS: That's Joan Bennett. She's explaining something to her husband. He don't believe her. The fink! [She smiles with an air of unutterable fatigue.]

[Some resolute-looking policemen enter followed by the cashier who speaks in an hysterical whisper.]

CASHIER: If anybody says "fire" it will cause a panic!

[The velvet rope is lifted and they go upstairs with flashlights. Gladys throws back her head. She laughs softly to herself. Then rather loudly and coarsely.]

BOY: What are you—l-laughing at?

GLADYS: She's always getting into some kind of a panic about things here, and you know why? The kids have so much fun in this place that it kills her! [Strolls up to the gilt nymph.] Lookit that naked lady! You like her shape? I bet *I* got a shape that's better than that. Big hips have gone out of style like horse-and-buggies! Haa-ha-ha-ha-haa- . . . Excuse me. I am going to get a drink of water. [*She enters the room marked "ladies."*]

[*The policemen come down with scraps of half-burned usher's outfit.*]

CASHIER [*following them*]: He must be crazy, that's all I've got to say, he must be crazy! Ripped off everything right here where I am standing! And burned it up there. I'm worried about Mr. Kroger. He had a hemorrhage of the bowels just two weeks ago from some malignant condition, and this has upset him so he's likely to have a set-back . . . .

[*The policemen have gone out with the half-incinerated garments.*]

CASHIER: Boy! Did Mr. Kroger come in while I was upstairs?

BOY: No, Ma'am.

CASHIER [*going out*]: Oh, Mr. Kroger! It's all right, Mr. Kroger! Everything is all right now, Mr. Kroger. It wasn't really a fire, it was just—

[*The outside door swings shut. Gladys comes back out of the ladies' room. She stands by the door staring at the new usher, slowly sweeping him up and down with her eyes. He turns his body at an angle away from her embarrassingly direct look.*]

BOY: —Wh-what time's it? It seems like I been standing here forever.

[*The girl laughs with huge indolence.*]

BOY: I don't like this place. I'm going to quit this job before I get fired. I don't like it. I don't like a place like this. I can't stand it here. I couldn't stand to stay here every afternoon. I'd go crazy. Things going on like this. My father told me to take this job but my mother wanted me not to. I should've listened to her and not to him but he's always nagging at me about being lazy. He thinks I'm lazy because I never worked in the summer before. But I did work. I wrote—I-I wrote—*poems!* —And had—*two*—p-published!

GLADYS: D'you know the song that goes "You're so Diff'rent from the Rest!"? That's my number, it's number eight on the juke-box at that place on the corner where we kids go nights . . . You will be going there nights if you stay here . . . [*Her voice is so indolent that it barely comes out.*]

[*Footsteps and voices are heard above. A policeman descends the stairs gripping Carl tightly by his arm.*]

CARL [*hoarsely*]: Nothing 'ud suit me better, nothing 'ud suit me better'n t' meet him in court! Let him talk. Let him do the talking. And then let me talk, too. We'll see who has the best story of what kind of place this is and what goes on here! [*As he is conducted outside.*] This is an evil place! This is a place full of evil!

[*The second officer flashes light momentarily on the gilt nymph at the base of the marble stairs. All go out except Gladys and the new usher.*]

GLADYS: Did you ever play truth or consequences?

BOY: —N-no!

GLADYS: I did last night. Somebody says "Heavy, heavy, hangs over your head, what shall the owner do to redeem it?" It was my best pair of stockings. And I had to answer the question. I can't repeat it to you. You'd be shocked to think that anybody would ask me that question! See that popcorn? That means she got upstairs! I'm going to find her! Want to follow? Come on up when the picture starts over again! [*Slips under the velvet rope and runs up the steps out of sight. From out of sight she calls down in a shrill whisper.*] Come on up when the picture starts over again!

[*The boy nods jerkily. After a moment he darts toward the steps and fastens the velvet rope back into place. Then he darts back to his formal position. He stands very straight and rigid and the music of the finale is heard rising to a spiritual climax. The boy's eyes stare straight out blue and glassy with wonder. With a jerky movement he swipes the sweat off his forehead.*]

SOMEONE ABOVE: *Sssssss! Sssssss!*

[*He bites his lips.*]

SOMEONE ABOVE: *Sssss! Sssssss! Sssss!*

[*He closes his eyes for a moment. The light starts fading. It lingers longest upon the gilt nymph.*]

CURTAIN

MISTER PARADISE

Mister Paradise was first performed at the Tennessee Williams/ New Orleans Literary Festival on March 17, 2005. It was directed by Perry Martin; the set design was by Chad Talkington; the costume design was by Trish McLain; the lighting design was by David Guidry. The cast, in order of appearance, was as follows:

THE GIRL	Leah Loftin
MISTER PARADISE	Dane Rhodes

Scene: A squalid residence in New Orleans's French Quarter.

GIRL: Mr. —*Paradise?*

[*Pause. He stares at her dumbly.*]

GIRL: Mr. —*Anthony* Paradise?

[*Mr. Paradise nods slowly as if confirming some awful truth. Her smile disappears completely by gradual degrees. She looks frightened and very uncertain: then opens her portfolio and produces a slender little volume of verse.*]

GIRL: This is your book?

MR. PARADISE: —Did you buy it?

GIRL: Yes.

MR. PARADISE: Then it belongs to *you.*

GIRL: No. [*With youthful conviction.*] A work of art is not a commodity, Mr. Paradise. It is never bought or sold. It always remains in the possession of the person who produced it. May I come in?

MR. PARADISE: —Yes.

[*He steps slowly aside to admit her. She pretends not to notice the intense disorder of Mr. Paradise's quarters.*]

GIRL: You received my letters?

MR. PARADISE: Yes.

GIRL: All three of them?

MR. PARADISE: Yes.

GIRL: Why didn't you answer my letters, Mr. Paradise?

[*He turns slowly and crosses to the window and opens the shutters.*]

MR. PARADISE: I have not heard the sound of Gabriel's horn.

GIRL: What do you mean?

MR. PARADISE: The time is not yet ripe for my resurrection. How did you happen to come across that little book?

GIRL: Mother and I were hunting antiques in the Quarter. We went in a little shop on Bourbon Street. There was a little Chinese tea-table with one leg slightly shorter than the others. The antique dealer had placed this volume under the short leg to balance the table. Mother bought the table. The chauffeur carried it out to the car. This little book was left there, lying on the floor. The antique dealer kicked it out of the way without looking at it. To me there is always something a little pathetic about a discarded book. You see, I write a little myself. Poems mostly. I know what it means to put your heart on paper. And have the paper lost or forgotten or—used to balance a table. I stooped over to look at the book. The title had been rubbed off, the gilt lettering was gone. But I saw your name still on it. Anthony—Paradise. It struck my fancy so I picked it up. I turned through the pages. "Why, this is a book of poems!" I said to the dealer. "Is it?" he said. "How did you get it?" I asked him. "Where did it come from? —How long has it been lying here? —Who is Anthony Paradise?" The antique dealer laughed. "God only knows," he said. "I probably bought it up with a bunch of others a long, long time ago. It might have been stuck in a bookcase I bought from somebody. Stuff like that don't sell. Sometimes I use it to light the fire up with!" "I'd like to buy it," I said. "How much do you want for this book?" He spread his arms in a great, munificent gesture and said, "You can have it for *nothing!*" The chauffeur came back in to remind me that mother was waiting in the car so I hurried back out, slipping the little volume of verse in my pocketbook. We rushed off to another cocktail party. I'm home from college for the holidays and life is a round of those things. It was more than usually dull this afternoon. I don't believe in dullness. I believe in excitement and wonder and passion. I believe in people having a storm in their hearts, a great big furious storm that sweeps all trivialities away like scraps of ribbons or dead leaves! —I went upstairs to look at the book which I suddenly remembered when somebody asked me how I liked Bryn Mawr for the twentieth time. Would you believe it? To my infinite wonder I discovered what I had been looking for exactly. A great big furious storm that swept those trivialities away like scraps of ribbon or—dead leaves! What do you think of that?

MR. PARADISE [*slowly*]: Are you referring to this book of verse?

GIRL: Yes—yes, yes!

MR. PARADISE: Hmmmm. Young lady, this book was published fifteen—twenty years ago. Nobody remembers it now. It's completely forgotten.

GIRL: *I* remember it. I sat up there in the powder-room for heaven knows how long. I read it through once more and then again and again. It was like—bells ringing inside me. Great big solemn cathedral bells that shook me through and through! Mother came upstairs. "Good gracious," she said. "Everyone thinks you've run away from the party! What on earth is the matter?" "Mother," I said. "Who is Mr. Anthony Paradise? Have you ever heard of a man named Paradise?" No, she hadn't and neither had anyone else. I went around feverishly enquiring of bookstores and libraries and all kinds of writers I know. No luck. Completely unknown. Then at last I wrote a letter to the publishing firm and in due time I received an answer saying that Mr. Anthony Paradise when last heard of was living in the old French Quarter of New Orleans but that was ten or fifteen years ago and it was feared that he might have disappeared altogether. Speaking of miracles, what do you think of that? Here you were, right at the tips of my fingers, me in one part of town and you in the other—fifteen minutes away. At first I thought of rushing right over without any warning. Time was so short, the holidays nearly over. I drove over here to this address which the publishers had given me and discovered that you still were actually in residence here and had been here for twenty years they told me. You weren't in. So I wrote you the first of the letters. I got no answer. Time came to go back to school. I pretended that I was ill. I faked a bad cold to postpone my departure and wrote you two more letters which you also ignored. I won't ask you why, it doesn't matter. Then I determined that I wouldn't be snubbed. I wouldn't let you refuse to be—discovered! So—so—so! Here I *am!* Here I am, Mr. Paradise, and here you *are!*

MR. PARADISE: Here you are, and here I am—yes, indeed. What are you intending to do about it?

GIRL: Oh, don't you know? Can't you guess? Mr. Paradise, I am going to give you back to the world!

MR. PARADISE: Give me back to the world?

GIRL: Yes, the stupid, blind, negligent world that let you slip away.

MR. PARADISE: Suppose I don't want to go back. Suppose I prefer to remain in oblivion, young lady.

GIRL: You can't, I won't let you! It's useless for you to resist! Don't try, Mr. Paradise, don't *try!* I've already set the ball in motion.

MR. PARADISE: Then stop it quickly, please.

GIRL: No. I've written letters to influential people, writers and publishers that I know in the East. I've already created a great deal of interest in you. When I leave here you're going to leave here with me.

MR. PARADISE: —No.

GIRL: Oh, yes, you are. You're going to live among people who appreciate genius. You're going to give readings and lectures.

MR. PARADISE: Readings? To whom?

GIRL: Clubs! Colleges! Societies of poets!

MR. PARADISE: Lectures? On what?

GIRL: Beauty! Art! Poetry!

MR. PARADISE: God forbid. Haven't you been reading the papers lately?

GIRL: Why?

MR. PARADISE: Today the world is interested in gunpowder. Poetry cannot compete with the sound of bursting shells. These are the times for the discovery of new weapons of destruction, not for the resurrection of neglected poets. Even if I wished to be resurrected, Gabriel has not yet blown the horn. The surest and cruelest way to destroy Anthony Paradise, the poet, is to exhibit Jonathan Jones, the man—or what is left of the man. Don't you see that? What a grisly spectacle I would present on a college lecture platform. Look at me! You're not blind. What do you see?

GIRL: The way you look doesn't matter.

MR. PARADISE: Oh, yes, it does. Maybe not to you, because you're young and generous. No, no, the time isn't ripe. Keep the book, remember my name, and watch the obituary column. Someday you will see the name of Jonathan Jones. Then come back again and look up Mr. Anthony Paradise. That will be his time—when Jones is dead. Jones is a living contradiction of Paradise. Paradise won't have a chance to breathe till Jones has stopped breathing. Take my word for that—and be satisfied.

GIRL: Can't you be Anthony Paradise now? Again?

MR. PARADISE: No. No, it's too late. I'm too old. Death is the only thing that can possibly save my reputation. Go back to school, little girl. There's an end to everything, even to supplies of gunpowder. When they're exhausted people will start looking again under broken table legs for little volumes of forgotten verse. By that time Jonathan Jones will be safely out of the way. The sun will be shining in a clean blue sky. Wind will stir the grass on the tops of hills. Children will dig in sand on sunny beaches. The world will be warm and serene and as young as tomorrow. Then all the old, sweet, gentle voices will be distinguished once again. You will hear wind in the trees and rain on the roof and the songs of long lost poets. Guns explode and destroy and are destroyed. But this— These little songs, however little and unimportant they are, they keep on singing forever. They have their times of eclipse. But they rise again. The motion of life is upwards, the motion of death is down. Only the blindest of all blind fools can fail to see which is going to be finally—highest up! Not death, but life, my dear. Life—*life!* I defy them to stop it forever! Not with all their guns, not with all their destruction! We will keep on singing. Someday the air all over the earth will be full of our singing.

[*A horn sounds.*]

MR. PARADISE: Is that your chauffeur?

GIRL: —Yes.

MR. PARADISE: You'd better go.

GIRL: Mr. Paradise—

MR. PARADISE: Yes?

GIRL: Maybe you're right. I'm going to do what you say, keep the book and remember your name—

MR. PARADISE: And watch the obituary column!

GIRL: —Yes. And when the time comes—you can depend on me, Mr. Paradise.

MR. PARADISE: Thank you, my dear. I shall *depend* on you.

GIRL: I promise you I won't fail you. Your future is safe in my hands– And now, Mr. Paradise—won't you kiss me goodbye?

MR. PARADISE: —No.

GIRL: Why not?

MR. PARADISE: No. —For the same reason that I wouldn't touch a clean white table cloth with—mud all over my fingers.

GIRL: —Oh. [*Gravely extends her hand.*] —Goodbye, Mr. Paradise.

CURTAIN

THE PALOOKA

The Palooka was first performed on October 2, 2003 by the Hartford Stage Company in Hartford, Connecticut. It was directed by Michael Wilson; the set design was by Jeff Cowie; the costume design was by David Woolard; the lighting design was by John Ambrosone; the original music and sound design were by Fitz Paton. The cast, in order of appearance, was as follows*:

THE PALOOKA	Kevin Geer
THE TRAINER	Remo Airaldi
THE KID	Curtis Billings

In the Hartford Stage production, the roles of THE PROMOTER and ANOTHER OLD BOXER were performed as offstage voices.

Discovered: Dressing room of a boxing arena. A small bare room containing a rubbing-table over which is suspended a green-shaded bulb. Air is blue with cigarette smoke.

On the table is seated the Palooka, a worn-out boxer in an old purple silk dressing robe. He looks grim and cynical. Beside him, on the bench, is a kid about to engage in his first professional match, very tense and eager. By the door, pacing restlessly is another old boxer.

PROMOTER [*entering with cigar*]: Awright, Jojo, you're on!

ANOTHER OLD BOXER: Okay. I'm comin. [*Swaggers out.*]

PALOOKA: He won't go more than two rounds.

TRAINER [*taping the kid's hands*]: Naw. He's too old. [*Rises.*] Excuse me, boys, I'm going to take a gander at this.

PALOOKA [*as the trainer leaves*]: Sure. They like to see an old palooka get knocked for a loop. Listen to 'em. They're yelling for murder. And they'll probably get it. The bastard's too old. He can't take it. Hand him one on the button and he'll fold. I guess you think that's funny, me calling another guy old. I'm not one of this year's kisses. Thirty-eight. In the insurance racket or selling bonds or anything else but the fighting game they'd say that you was still young at thirty-eight. But when a fighter's that old he's a worn-out palooka. He starts talking funny, dodging things that ain't there. And the crowds yell at him like that cause they want to see him knocked out cold. Maybe five or ten years ago he was their hero, their favorite boxer. What the hell do they care now? [*Pause.*] Why don't you say something, kid? Are you nervous?

KID: Yeah.

PALOOKA: Don't be nervous. Whatcha got to be nervous about?

KID: This here's my first pro bout.

PALOOKA: What of it? You got what it takes. You're young.

KID: I got no experience, have I?

PALOOKA: Naw, you ain't got no glass chin yet.

KID: If I don't make good they'll never give me another match.

PALOOKA: That's the attitude, kid. Do or die. Who you fighting?

KID: Blackie Shaw.

PALOOKA: Him? That slap-happy palooka? [*Gives a "bird."*] You'll bust him into the middle of next week!

KID: Know him, do you?

PALOOKA: I seen him fight.

KID: He's plenty big, ain't he.

PALOOKA: Plenty of beef, yeah, but no form, no technique. For you it's a breeze, a push-over!

KID: Zat so?

PALOOKA: He's a sucker for a left uppercut. Leaves himself wide open. You wade right in there and hang one under his jaw right here or in the breadbasket. And he'll fold his tents like the Arabs.

KID: I guess you know a good deal about boxing.

PALOOKA: I seen lots a fights in my time. From inside and outside the ring. I've known some real scrappers.

[*Kid rises and starts pacing floor.*]

PALOOKA [*lighting a cigarette*]: Take it easy. What's the use of burnin' shoe leather? Sit down. —Ever heard of a palooka named Galveston Joe?

KID: Sure. He wasn't no palooka. He used to be the light heavy-weight champ.

PALOOKA: [*with slight smile*]: Yeah. He wasn't no palooka.

KID: You know he wasn't.

PALOOKA: Know what's become of that guy?

KID: Him? I don't know. I guess he must've quit fighting by now.

PALOOKA: Retired? Yeah. He's lined his pockets with lotsa mozooma. Made lots of dough.

KID: Sure. He was a big-timer. A swell guy, too. Everyone liked him.

PALOOKA: When was the last you heard of him?

KID: Oh, I don't know. When I was a kid selling papers. He was my hero then. Galveston Joe, I had his picture pasted up in my bedroom—

PALOOKA: Did ya?

KID: —and I used to stand up in front of it and square off and imagine myself like him, the light heavy-weight champ.

PALOOKA: Why not? You're going places.

KID: I remember the time when he come into town for his match with the Mexican Puma.

PALOOKA: Yeah, the Puma. That was a breeze for him.

KID: God, how the kids mobbed the station! Musta been thousands of 'em shoutin for Galveston Joe. And the women, too.

PALOOKA [*dreamily*]: Yeah, the women.

KID: Fightin' to get up to him.

PALOOKA: Kissin' him an' beggin' for him to sign his name. Jerkin' buttons off his coat. Snatchin' his green carnation.

KID: Green?

PALOOKA: He was Irish you know.

KID: You seen it?

PALOOKA: Naw, but I can imagine. You see, I used to know him.

KID [*eagerly*]: Didja?

PALOOKA: I guess I did. Useda work in his corner. I used to give him the sponge.

KID: God! It'd be an honor to give *him* the sponge.

PALOOKA: Honor? Hell, it was a privilege, boy!

KID: Say! I sure would like to have been a friend of Galveston's. He sure had something about him that—

PALOOKA: Yeah. Lotsa *glamour*. That's what they call it in Hollywood.

KID: That's it. Glamour.

PALOOKA: Lived like the King of Siam. Stopped at the best hotels and always traveled in a drawing-room. Spent money like water. Best accommodations was never too good for old Joe. Generous too. Ask him for a ten spot— Go on! Take half a grand!

KID: Where is he now I wonder? You know? [*Pause.*]

PALOOKA: Sure. Sout' America.

KID: Yeah?

PALOOKA: Yeah, he's made a big fortune down there. Oil business. That's why you don't hear him mentioned so much any more. He's retired from the fighting game and made good on Wall Street. I mean on the – Argentine board of trade. He's got a monopoly on natural gas or something down there.

KID: Jeez! Think of that! It ain't surprising, though.

PALOOKA: Naw. Nothing that Galveston Joe could do would be surprising. He was that kind of guy.

KID: Still is? Is he?

PALOOKA: Sure! Why not? You oughta see the stations now when he comes into town!

KID: Crowds?

PALOOKA: Crowds! They tear the place down. Have to build a new depot every time he takes a trip. Kids yelling his name.

Galveston! Galveston Joe! [*Half rises.*] And the women—fighting like wild-cats to get a button off his vest or snatch the green carnation from his lapel or—God a'mighty, I tell you the fans go wild!

KID [*dreamily*]: Jeez! It's sort of—inspirational—that's right. That's the word for it. To think of a guy getting famous like that. Celebrated!

PALOOKA: You bet.

KID: I guess he was just a young punk like me to start with.

PALOOKA: Uh-huh. The same as you are.

KID: And now just look where he is!

PALOOKA: Just look where he's got to now!

KID: Lissen!

PALOOKA: Yes, the fight's over! They musta murdered the stiff! Awight! You butchers! I'm on next! —And then you . . . .

KID: Me?

PALOOKA: Your big moment kid. —How you feel?

KID: Swell!

PALOOKA: You tell 'em. Do like I told you. Wade right in there the first round and hang one right under his jaw like this or in the bread basket. You'll bust that palooka into the middle of next week—

TRAINER [*entering quickly*]: Awight, you're on, there! C'mon, c'mon let's keep this show moving.

PALOOKA: Okay. I'm comin'. [*Walks slowly, lifelessly through the door.*]

TRAINER [*with a hard laugh*]: He means he's going. To the slaughter! Lissen to 'em yelling out there.

KID [*awed*]: What for?

TRAINER: That new *monicker* of his don't fool the old-timers. *They* know him.

KID: *Know* him?

TRAINER: Sure. *They* recognize Galveston Joe.

KID: Galveston—Joe!

TRAINER: Yeah, the biggest *has-been* in the racket. Lissen to 'em yelling! They love it! Like feeding Christians to the lions—This won't take long. The Palooka's got a glass chin! How are you feeling, sonny? Okay?

KID [*slowly*]: Yes. I'm feeling okay.

[*Roars continue. Black out.*]

CURTAIN

ESCAPE

Escape was first performed at the Tennessee Williams/New Orleans Literary Festival on March 17, 2005. It was directed by Perry Martin; the set design was by Chad Talkingon; the costume design was by Trish McLain; the lighting design was by David Guidry. The cast, in order of appearance, was as follows:

BIG   Fred Plunkett
STEVE   Jamal Dennis
TEXAS   Tony Molina

Scene: The bunk-house of a southern chain-gang, about twilight of a summer evening. It is lighted by a coal-oil lamp that swings from the ceiling and is surrounded by a swarm of night insects. Outside we hear the song of locusts, faint and monotonous, and the distant baying of hounds. The group has a hunched, expectant appearance as they sit around the plain, bare wooden table. There is a deck of much-thumbed cards which they nervously finger throughout the play.

BIG: You reckon he's got to the hollow?

STEVE: Naw, not yit.

TEXAS: It's my opinion he ain't gonna git very far.

BIG: We'll take your opinion faw what it's worth.

STEVE: Lissen them hounds.

TEXAS: Lawd, I'd hate to hear them shaggin' my footsteps!

BIG: I betcha that Billy ain't scared.

TEXAS: That nigger ain't got sense enough to be scared.

BIG: Shut up.

STEVE: Texas, cain't you evuh forgit a grudge?

TEXAS: I ain't holdin' a grudge. I'm pullin' faw him same's you all.

BIG: Say that on Sunday!

STEVE: Texas ain't forgot how Billy kicked his behime faw squealin' on de jack-pot.

BIG: I wish Billy ain't tried this here. It's takin' too big a chancet. He on'y had seven mo' months t'go.

TEXAS: It's like I said. He ain't got sense no mo'n a jack-rabbit.

BIG: Shut up. Was that the Cannonball?

STEVE: Naw.

BIG: What was it then?

STEVE: Thunder. It ain't time faw the Cannonball yit.

BIG: How long?

STEVE: I figger it's twenty, thuty minutes yit till she be comin' thru'.

BIG: Tha's too long.

TEXAS: Way too long.

BIG: Shut up.

STEVE: Shut up, you crepe-hanger.

TEXAS: I jus' repeatin' what you said.

BIG: You keep you mouth outa this.

STEVE: Well, them hounds're stopped. He's thown 'em plum off.

BIG: Sounds like they still down the East fork o' the Sunflower.

STEVE: That's where they are.

BIG: An' ole Billy's prob'ly swum back up the west fork. He kin swim like a fish.

TEXAS: Dey prob'ly split up an some take de east fork an' some take de west. Cap'n ain't nobody's fool.

BIG: You gonna be somebody's cawpse if you don' shut up.

STEVE: Draw a card, Big.

[*Big draws one.*]

STEVE: What you got?

BIG: Tray of clubs.

STEVE: Mmm.

BIG: What's that?

STEVE: Two hawses an' a wagon all of 'em black.

TEXAS: Oughta be four black spots includin' Billy!

BIG: If I pull a knife on you, black boy, you ain't gonna see it. It's gonna be buried too deep in your stinkin' hide.

TEXAS: I ain't readin' the cards!

BIG: Cards don' mean a thing. I known a gal could read past an' future like a book right in a man's eyeballs. She seen chain-gain fo' me six weeks fo' I got—Lissen!

STEVE: Sounds like the hounds took a new start.

BIG: They're kitin' west like blue Judas!

STEVE [*going to the barred window*]: I kin see lights down in the hollow.

BIG [*joining him*]: Yeah. Almos' down to the trestle.

[*Train whistle blows.*]

BIG: There she's blowin! Come on, Billy!

TEXAS: It's too late. They got him headed off now.

BIG: Shut yer goddam trap!

[*He shoves him away from window.*]

STEVE: Lissen—she's slowin' down faw the grade.

BIG: Now Billy's chancet!

[*Gunfire is heard.*]

BIG: Wha's that?

STEVE: You know what that is, Big Boy!

TEXAS: Curtains faw Billy!

BIG: There it goes again. Three, four shots!

STEVE: Maybe he's givin' 'em a run faw their money.

TEXAS: He's packin' a gut full of lead!

BIG [*flashing a razor*]: Maybe you'd like to pack some of this!

TEXAS: Stay way frum me wit' that razor or I'll—

BIG [*advancing*]: You'll what?

TEXAS: Stay 'way frum me wit' that thing!

STEVE: Lay off him Big.

BIG: I'll carve my sign on his belly if ever I git him out some-wheres in the open!

STEVE: It's all over now. Cannonball's gone. When I seen that tray of clubs I known whichaway Billy was goin'.

BIG: Don be too quick with the coffin. You ain't seen him laid in it yet.

STEVE: Truck's comin' up this way. —Stopped at the commis-sary.

BIG: Kin you see anything?

STEVE: Yeah.

BIG: What?

STEVE: Takin' something out the back end.

BIG [*after a pause*]: Turn the lamp out. We mought as well git to bed.

STEVE: He's free, dat's how I look at it. Billy's free.

BIG: Yeah. He's free.

CURTAIN

WHY DO YOU SMOKE SO MUCH, LILY?

(A SHORT STORY IN ONE ACT)

Why Do You Smoke So Much, Lily? was first performed in Chicago, Illinois by The Dream Engine Theatre Company on January 19, 2007. It was directed by John Zajac; the set, costumes and lights were designed by Doug Valenta; the stage manager was Nazan Kayali; and the stage hand was Brent Collins. The cast, in order of appearance, was as follows:

MRS. YORKE	Mary Mikva
LILY	Leslie Frame
YOUNG MAN	Troy Slavens

Scene: *A fashionable apartment in the west end of Saint Louis.*

Mrs. Yorke stands before a long oval mirror in the living room. Her every movement is replete with the rather gruesome vanity of stout middle age. She pats her marcelled hair and preens herself fatuously this way and that. Her pendulous bosom heaves. Her hands flutter about like puffy white pigeons and her heavy bracelets and ear-pendants jangle like the harness of a trotting pony.

MRS. YORKE: They set the waves too close last time, don't you think?

[*Lily says nothing. She sits smoking in the sunroom. She looks slightly dazed. Her eyes stare vacantly into the brackish aquarium where tiny fish like animated bits of coral and mother-of-pearl eddy ceaselessly through their rock castles and forests of floating green weeds.*]

MRS. YORKE [*lifting her voice and turning her eyes*]: I said they set the waves too close last time, don't you think?

[*Lily stirs slightly on the wicker settee and exudes another transparent grey cone from her pursed lips. She seems neither to see nor hear her mother.*]

MRS. YORKE [*glaring*]: Why do you smoke so much, Lily? It's making you dull!

LILY [*her eyes taking color, a brilliant, tortured green*]: Good heavens, mother! What else can I do?

MRS. YORKE [*fretfully primping*]: There's plenty of useful things for a young girl to do. You could take up knitting. It's gotten frightfully smart. All of this year's girls were knitting at Susan

Holt's tea. They sat all around the floor with their knitting bags and their needles, and it looked too cunning for words!

LILY [*laughing sharply*]: I'm not one of this year's girls. With a couple of knitting needles and a woolen bag on my knees I'd make a perfect picture of the resigned spinster!

MRS. YORKE [*bristling*]: Listen here, young lady, you've got to snap out of that old-maid complex! You've only been out five years. That isn't forever. Of course I'd always wished . . . .

LILY [*closing her tortured eyes and inhaling deeply from the cigarette*]: I know, mother! You wished me to get married my first year out. You wished me to get married my second year out. My third and fourth years out you wished me to get married . . . .

MRS. YORKE [*applying rouge*]: Sure I wished you to get married! What mother doesn't wish her daughter to get married? What else is there for you to do? The way things are now . . . .

LILY [*bitterly*]: I know, I know! Our money's all gone!

MRS. YORKE [*working powder-puff angrily*]: All gone is right! We're at our rope's end!

LILY [*laughing harshly and lighting a new cigarette*]: But I won't get married, mother! Nobody's asked me! What do you expect me to do? Club some innocent male and drag him into my boudoir? It isn't legal mother! There's a law against rape in Missouri!

MRS. YORKE: Stop that vulgar talk!

LILY: I'm just telling you the plain facts! Nobody's asked me!

[*Lily's laughter jerks painfully between puffs at her trembling cigarette. She seems to be trying to stop her laughter with smoke, like water splashed futilely over a blazing fire. The laughter keeps on. It shakes her thin body.*]

MRS. YORKE [*applying lipstick*]: You've got only yourself to blame! Heaven knows I did everything that a mother could do. I devoted my life to preparing you for society. I never made a single misstep. You went to the best private school in the city. You went to the best finishing school in the East. You took the most expensive European tour. You met all the right people. All the eligible young men . . . .

LILY: All the eligible young men? You mean the pink-faced dandies! God, how I hated them! I stepped on their toes just to hear how they'd squeal!

MRS. YORKE [*jangling furiously from the mirror to the sun-room door*]: I don't doubt it! You and your intellectual nonsense! Enough to scare any sensible man clean out of his wits! They don't want a walking book-report, Lily! They want flesh and blood! Why don't you try acting dumb for a change? Just sit there and say nothing! Give them a chance to get started themselves . . . .

LILY: I'm surprised you don't suggest that I try a little old-fashioned bundling!

MRS. YORKE: You know very well what I mean!

LILY [*writhing*]: Sure, I know what you mean! Only it makes me feel sick at my stomach! Refined, high-society prostitution! Here is my body! Take off my clothes and climb on! All I demand is a legal contract and lots of cold cash!

MRS. YORKE [*hoarsely*]: Shut up! Shut up! You ought to have your mouth washed out with soap for talking like that! [*Snatches magazine from Lily's lap and tosses it to the floor.*] You've been reading too much filthy fiction! I'm going to take all of these trashy, new-fangled magazines of yours and pitch them out the back window! Who reads that kind of stuff? Bohemians, Bolsheviks, Bohunks, long-haired Russians, and what not!

[*Lily's laughter dies of breathlessness. The cigarette still hangs from her lips. Mrs. Yorke leans over and snatches it away. She tosses it into the aquarium.*]

MRS. YORKE: Quit that damned smoking! Everywhere I turn there's dead butts! All over the house! Yesterday I found myself sitting on one . . .

LILY [*covering her face with both hands*]: That's a crude pun, mother.

MRS. YORKE [*failing to catch the joke*]: Crude? *Crude?* Ah, you're the *crude* one, Lily! Honestly, if you . . .

[*The telephone rings from the rear of the apartment and Mrs. Yorke jangles off, leaving only a strong scent of hyacinths to adulterate the relief of her absence. Lily lights another cigarette. She exhales the smoke with a loud sigh. Presses the palm of one hand hard against her forehead, rapidly shaking her head and twisting her lips down with pain.*]

MRS. YORKE [*talking to hair-dresser over the phone*]: You can take me now? Oh, dear, I'll come right over!

LILY [*laughing weakly*]: Thank God, she's getting out!

[*Mrs. Yorke returns to the front in her seal-skin coat, velvet toque, and black kid gloves. The coat is new. She preens herself again before the long mirror, pursing her wrinkled lips and arching her plucked eyebrows.*]

MRS. YORKE [*raptly*]: How does it look?

LILY [*with eyes closed*]: It looks like rain.

MRS. YORKE [*angrily pulling at her toque*]: I wish you'd show a little more intelligence when I speak to you, Lily!

LILY [*slightly shaking with hoarse laughter*]: If I did I'd stuff my ears with cotton!

[*The taxi is honking outside. Mrs. Yorke bustles to the door.*]

MRS. YORKE [*turning toward Lily as she leaves*]: I wish you'd quit smoking so much! It's ruining your skin, simply ruining your
. . . .

[*The door slams on her voice. Lily sways slightly on the couch as if drunk. She rises stiffly to her feet and begins to wander aimlessly around the five-room apartment. She scatters ashes wherever she walks. When the cigarette is half-consumed she extinguishes it against the paneled wall of the dining room and deposits the butt on a serving-tray. Then she lights another. She retires to her own room. Its furnishings are ivory and the curtains and bedspread are pink. Lily herself is dark and sallow. Her features are biggish. Her body long and angular. She would make a rather good-looking young man.*

She stands in the center of the pink and ivory room and draws upon the cigarette. Her fingers start shaking again. She presses her hand to her forehead and gasps sharply. The cigarette slips from her fingers and plops to the floor. She grinds it beneath her heel and lights another. Puffing voraciously, she sinks down on the bed. Its softness makes her more restless. She gets up, still smoking, and walks around the room some more. She pauses in front of the vanity and looks into its huge polished mirrors. She grins and simpers at her reflection.

Automatically her lips begin to mumble certain phrases which are most familiar to her mother's lips at social gatherings they have attended together. At first she speaks the words aloud. Then she seems to become frightened. She falls back from the mirror. She clamps both hands over her mouth and then over her ears. But the voice which she has created cannot be stemmed even though her own lips are now quiet. Its ghostly whisper goes on, in the simpering, falsetto tone which her mother employs on social occasions.]

VOICE: Lily's a most unusual child. She's really very much like her poor father. He was the intellectual type, too, you know. Quite interested in writing. Dear Stephen! He had to give it up, of course, when we got married. But he kept all his old papers. Kept them locked up in his desk. I'll never forget the fuss that he made when I burned them. He cried like a baby. Poor, *dear* Stephen! A brilliant man. But he had *such* an impractical nature before our marriage. I cured him of that. He came around beautifully after the first few years. I managed nearly all his affairs. Lily's just like him, dear child! It's just a stage that she'll have to pass through, this intellectual nonsense. Sooner or later she'll be wanting a home and children, of course, like all the other young girls, and I'm sure, quite *sure*, that she'll make some man an *awfully* good wife!

[Lily extinguishes her cigarette against a spot in the mirror— which reflects one of her eyes. She opens the drawer of the vanity, takes out a silver case, presses it open, removes another cigarette and flicks the lighter.]

LILY *[whimpering like a tired child]*: Father . . . *father* . . . why did you have to leave me like this?

[She springs suddenly from the chair. Slams both doors. Locks them. Throws herself face downwards upon the bed.]

LILY [*passionately*]: Father, she's getting me like she did you! She's *killing* me, father! Did you hear her last night? I tell you . . . .

[*The counterpane catches fire from the cigarette. She slaps it out and gets up.*]

LILY [*laughing wildly*]: Oh, my God! I've gone crazy!

[*She gasps and looks toward the locked doors. Through all the rooms of the silent apartment she seems to hear the fretful ghost of her mother's voice bearing in upon her again: quietly at first, then with a deafening shrillness.*]

VOICE [*slow and whining*]: Why do you smoke so much, Lily? It's ruining your skin! Lily, your complexion's getting sallow! [*The voice grows more piercing.*] Look at your fingers, Lily! They're yellow as a Chinaman's! And your teeth! Good HEAV-ENS! Tobacco stains all over them! [*The voice becomes like a fist banging at the door.*] Lily, Lily! Why do you smoke so much? It's wrecking your nerves! That's why you're cross all the time! You can't sleep! You act like you're losing your mind! It's those damned cigarettes that do it! Those damned cigarettes! That's why you can't sleep nights! It's wrecking your nerves! Oh, it's no use wasting money on nerve-specialists, Lily, when you keep up this eternal smoking! Smoking, smoking, smoking! All the time, Lily!

[*She lifts her hands to her eyes and shuts her eyes tight.*]

LILY: Oh, mother, I wish you'd keep *still*!

[*The cigarette burns the tips of her fingers. She crushes it out and hastily, almost frantically, lights another. She tries to concentrate on the stillness of the vacant rooms outside. There is really no voice. Her mother is gone. The rooms outside are empty. But through all their emptiness the remembered voice still pulses like the nerves of her cigarette-burned fingers.*]

VOICE: What haven't I done for you, Lily! I've sent you to the most exclusive schools. You took the most expensive European tour. Thousands of dollars spent on your debut. I saw that you met the right people. All the eligible men in town. Lived way beyond our means. Went into debt. Just to give you the proper background, Lily. The best advantages. But it can't go on forever. You aren't getting any younger, you know. You'll have to perk up. You don't have to be pretty. Just smile. Play *up* to them, Lily. Let them see that you've got some life in your bones. *That's* what they want! Play *up* to them, play *up* to them Lily! God knows that *I've* done all I can!

[*Lily is really frightened now. She buries her face in her hands and claws at her forehead. The cigarette falls unnoticed on the ivory top of the dresser and burns a brown scar. In the outside hall she hears footsteps. The key turns in the lock and the stout, middle-aged woman, breathing heavily, trundles into the front of the apartment. It is her mother returning from the beauty parlor. It is her mother, scented with hyacinth, freshly marcelled. Instantly she begins to sniff at the blue-tinted air.*]

MRS. YORKE [*screaming at the top of her voice*]: Lily! *Lily!* The house is simply *filled* with smoke and ashes!

CURTAIN

SUMMER AT THE LAKE

Summer at the Lake was first performed under the title *Escape* by the Shakespeare Theatre on April 22, 2004 at the Kennedy Center in Washington D.C. It was directed by Michael Kahn; the set design was by Andrew Jackness; the costume design was by Catherine Zuber; the lighting design was by Howell Binkley; the sound design was by Martin Desjardins; and original music was composed by Adam Wernick. The cast, in order of appearance, was as follows:

DONALD FENWAY, a boy of about seventeen	Cameron Folmar
MRS. FENWAY, a fretful middle-aged woman	Joan van Ark
ANNA, an elderly servant	Kathleen Chalfant

Scene: The living room of a summer cottage. The walls are white varnished and glaring with afternoon sun. The furniture is wicker. Mrs. Fenway lies propped up on the settee. She is a heavy woman in lavender linen with dark perspiration stains about the arm-pits. Several strings of gaudy beads hang about her throat. She continually mops her forehead with a crumpled handkerchief. Her hair hangs fuzzily over her forehead. On the floor are movie-magazines and a pitcher of ice water.

Donald bears no resemblance to his mother. He is a thin sensitive youth who moves about the room as though searching for something.

MRS. FENWAY [*irritably*]: What makes you so restless, Donald?

DONALD: Nothing

MRS. FENWAY: Then sit still! I can't bear to see you wandering around in that aimless way. Get you a book and read it.

DONALD: I'm tired of books.

MRS. FENWAY: I thought you could never get tired of books!

DONALD: There's nothing in them but words.

MRS. FENWAY: What would you expect to find in them?

DONALD: Well, I'm tired of them.

MRS. FENWAY: You're being petulant. I must say it isn't very manly of you when you see the condition that I am in. I'm simply prostrated. What's the use of leaving the city when it's this hot on the lake?

DONALD: You'll be back soon enough.

MRS. FENWAY: Oh, heavens! What was it your father said in the letter?

DONALD: He said he hoped your nervous condition was better.

MRS. FENWAY: I don't mean that, you know what I mean. Something about money.

DONALD: Have you forgotten?

MRS. FENWAY: Give it here. [*She takes the letter.*] I can't make it out, it's all so jumbled, and my head goes around like a top.

DONALD: He says the season's been cut short and we'll have to come home the sixteenth. He's planning to sell the cottage. And there's something about me taking a job in the wholesale business.

MRS. FENWAY: Absurd! But I suppose we'll have to come home. That's tiresome.

DONALD: Yes.

MRS. FENWAY [*petulantly*]: I don't want to go home. It's hot here but heaven knows it's better than that stifling apartment will be. And him wanting me to move into a cheaper place. The nerve of it. I'll lay you ten to one he's keeping a mistress. What did I do with the Empirin tablets? I can't stand this headache another moment without screaming out loud and I have to play bridge with the Vincents at half-past four. Where are they? Donald!

DONALD: What?

MRS. FENWAY: Why do you stand there looking like that?

DONALD: Like what?

MRS. FENWAY: Like you were lost all the time.

DONALD: Is that how I look?

MRS. FENWAY: Yes. Have you fallen in love?

DONALD: No.

MRS. FENWAY: I wish you had. Then there might be some excuse for your acting so queerly. It's no wonder you don't make friends. People think you're foolish when you go around looking like that. You ought to try and cultivate more—Donald! Where are you going?

DONALD: I'm going out on the lake for awhile.

MRS. FENWAY: No. Don't.

DONALD: Why not?

MRS. FENWAY: You're out there too much. You leave me alone all the time and I don't know where you are.

DONALD: On the lake.

MRS. FENWAY: Yes, but you stay so long and it's hot and my head swims. You don't have to go rushing off every time I open my mouth to say something.

DONALD [*sitting down again*]: I'm sorry.

MRS. FENWAY: No, you aren't. You aren't sorry about a thing. You're indifferent, that's what. All you care about is mooning around out there on the lake. And you're nearly grown. You'll have to wake up pretty soon and take things more seriously. You can't just dream your whole life away. Now that your father and I have separated things won't be easy, you know. I shall probably have to take up a teaching contract or something though heaven knows how I shall manage, what with my head swimming as it does all the time and my misplaced vertebra and—Tell Anna to be sure and iron my white linen waist. It's nearly four already. Do you hear me?

DONALD: Yes.

MRS. FENWAY: Is that all you have to say to me ever. Just "Yes"?

DONALD [*rising and going to window*]: What do you want me to say to you? Tell me and I'll say it!

MRS. FENWAY [*leaning back on sofa*]: Oh, hush. The heat in here is terrific. I see black spots in front of my eyes again this afternoon. I suppose I'll have to take up my chiropractic treatments again as soon as I get back to the city. When I think of returning to that dreadful apartment in the middle of August it makes my head swim. I guess we should have stayed on McPherson where at least we had southern exposure. And now him having the nerve to suggest I find a place that rents cheaper! He says he thinks with just the two of us he thinks I might dispense with the maid. Wants me to get rid of Anna! Isn't that what he said?

DONALD: Yes

MRS. FENWAY: He knows I couldn't exist without Anna. He said that just to provoke me. Where did I put those Empirin tablets? Anna's always sticking things around in odd places. Getting old and absent-minded. See if she could have stuck them behind the tea service. *Do you hear me, Donald?*

DONALD: Yes. What did you say?

MRS. FENWAY: Oh! Me lying helpless with a splitting head and you just floating off into space! [*She calls.*] Anna!

[*After a moment the old woman shuffles in.*]

ANNA: Yes?

MRS. FENWAY: Where's my Empirin?

ANNA: In your handbag. You want one?

MRS. FENWAY: Yes.

[*Anna goes out and returns with a tablet.*]

MRS. FENWAY: I don't know how I shall ever pull myself together for this bridge game. If I didn't know it was necessary for me to have some diversion I would just call the whole thing off. Mrs. Vincent is such a bore since she's taken up mysticism. She gets messages now from cousins five or six generations back. I don't believe a word of it! Anna. You won't forget to iron my white linen waist?

ANNA [*as she goes out*]: No, ma'am.

MRS. FENWAY: She's getting so dull. No, ma'am, yes, ma'am: Always the same tone of voice. [*Picking up the letter.*] Your father says here you'd best not make any plans for entering college this Fall since the—

DONALD. Don't!

MRS. FENWAY What?

DONALD: Read any more of it!

MRS. FENWAY: Yes, that's you. You can't stand to face anything disagreeable. You want to go on being a child all your life. Well, you'll find out soon enough that it can't be done. You'll have to start taking on some responsibilities now that your father's cut loose and gotten involved more than likely with some cheap woman!

DONALD: I don't have to do anything I don't want to do! [*He rises and goes over to the window again.*] I don't have to be anything but just what I am! [*He faces her desperately.*] Oh, God, mother, I don't want to go home! I hate it! I hate it! It's like being caught in a hideous trap! [*He covers his face and sits down on the window sill.*] The brick walls and the concrete and the—the black fire-escapes! It's them I hate most of all—fire-escapes! Don't they think people who live in apartments need to escape from anything besides fire?

MRS. FENWAY: Donald! I wish you'd stop talking queerly!

DONALD: I dreamed I was on one last night.

MRS. FENWAY: On what?

DONALD: A fire-escape. An endless black fire-escape. I kept running and running, up it and down it, and I never got anywhere! At last I stopped running, I couldn't run any further, and the black iron thing started twisting around me like a snake! I couldn't breathe!

MRS. FENWAY: Stop it! In my nervous condition it's a crime to make me listen to stuff like that! What did you eat before going to bed last night?

DONALD [*laughing sharply*]: Yes, blame it on my digestion! — I'm going out.

MRS. FENWAY: Where to?

DONALD: I told you. The lake.

MRS. FENWAY: Always the lake! And by yourself, too—it's not normal! Before you go remind Anna once more about my white linen waist. She's probably forgotten and— Oh, Donald! Before you go out I wish you would clean my white kid slippers.

DONALD [*absently*]: Your white kid slippers?

MRS. FENWAY: Yes. Will you do that for mother? [*She rises.*] I'd do it myself but I'm just too exhausted. This heat makes my head go around like a top. Goodness! I have a blister right on the ball of my foot! Don't we get the *Saturday Evening Post* anymore? [*She pushes the damp hair back from her forehead.*] I really ought to stay in, the lake is so glaring, it's just sure to make me dizzy walking along the drive. I don't see why we ever got a cottage so far out of the way. Where's the *True Story*? I promised Mrs. Vincent I'd let her have it. Donald! Pull that shade down! The lake is so glaring it hurts my eyes.

DONALD [*obeying*]: Anything else I can do for you?

MRS. FENWAY: No, but you won't forget the kid slippers?

DONALD: I'll fix them later.

MRS. FENWAY: Always later. You're like your father in that respect. Procrastination about all things. Well, time doesn't wait for people. [*She pours a glass of water and flops down again on the divan.*] It just keeps going along. You'll find that out for yourself some day.

DONALD: Time? I don't care about time. Time's nothing.

MRS. FENWAY: Time is one thing that nobody ever gets away from.

DONALD: I do. I've gotten away from it.

MRS. FENWAY: Have you indeed!

DONALD: Yes, on the lake. There isn't any time out there. It's night or morning or afternoon but it's never any particular time.

MRS. FENWAY: Donald!

[*Donald turns toward her slowly.*]

MRS. FENWAY: I don't like to hear you talk like that. Young people don't say crazy things like that. It sounds like you were—different—or queer or something. Don't be like that, Donald. It isn't fair to your mother. People will say that you're not like the other boys and they'll—they'll avoid you. You'll find yourself being left out of things all around. And you won't like that. I want you to learn to be normal and sociable and able to—to take your place in the world. Myself, I'm a nervous wreck and your father, he always has been one of these fly-up-the-creeks, but you, Donald, you've got to be a strong, responsible man!

DONALD [*after a pause*]: Don't worry about me.

MRS. FENWAY: I want you to grow up, Donald. Do you understand?

DONALD: Yes.

MRS. FENWAY: I'm sure that isn't too much for your mother to ask. What became of that letter? I suppose I shall have to try and concentrate on the thing and see what he's driving at. It's all so jumbled. Some thing about the concert season being cut short and the [*she begins reading snatches aloud*]—"the season cut short— returning—hope that your—nervous condition is better"— hmm—"vacate the cottage by the sixteenth as it must be sold— must be—yes, sold!"—hmmm— [*She turns several pages quickly. Donald slips out.*] —"keeping separate establishments in the city—expenses so great—Donald perhaps can get a position with the Lanchester Wholesale firm—time that the boy settles down and—hmmm—let me know your decision—make plans— hmmm—" Oh, Lord—make plans—I can't make any plans. [*She looks up and notices Donald is gone.*] Donald! *Donald.* [*She takes off her glasses and leans back, fanning her sweating face with the letter.*] WHEW! [*She leans over and removes a garter which has left a red circle about her leg. She rubs it and groans. Then leans forward with a cross look on her face.*] Anna! [*Pause. She rises angrily.*] Anna! COME HERE!

ANNA [*entering*]: Did you call, Ma'am?

MRS. FENWAY: Yes, who did you think!—

ANNA: What d'you want, Ma'am?

MRS. FENWAY [*pausing*]: Heavens! I can't remember!

[*Anna starts to shuffle out again.*]

MRS. FENWAY: Oh, yes, my white linen waist. I have to wear it over to the Vincents' at four-thirty. What time is it now?

ANNA: Fifteen of five.

MRS. FENWAY: Heavens, I'll never make it on time! Anna, I wish you would try to remind me about my engagements. I don't think it's asking too much.

ANNA: Yes, ma'am.

MRS. FENWAY: And the shoes. I told Donald to clean them but he's gone out again on the lake. Anna, sit down. What do you think of him going out on the lake like that?

ANNA. [*seating herself*]: He's out there most of the time, Mrs. Fenway.

MRS. FENWAY: Yes, most of the time. It's not natural. I'm afraid he's a dreamer.

ANNA: Yes ma'am, that's what he is.

MRS. FENWAY: Yes, a dreamer. One of those impractical persons like his father and I had so hoped he'd turn out different.

ANNA: They say that still water runs deep.

MRS. FENWAY: Yes, deep under the ground where nobody can see it! [*Pause.*] I don't like that, Anna. I want him to be a normal young man.

ANNA: He's a strange one.

MRS. FENWAY: Worse than his father ever was and that's saying a lot.

ANNA: Maybe he needs to be put in a good private school, Mrs. Fenway.

MRS. FENWAY: On what? Anna, we've got no more money. In

this letter my husband tells me the concert season's cut short and he'll be without funds till the middle of October. It means we come home the sixteenth and stew in that hot little apartment the rest of the summer. Open that window, Anna. No wonder it's so stifling in here, we've got the lake breeze cut off. —Can you see Donald?

ANNA. [*at the window*]: He's going down the wharf in his trunks.

MRS. FENWAY: Has he got the oars?

ANNA: No.

MRS. FENWAY: Then he's swimming. That's better. He won't stay out so long swimming— Maybe I'll call off my engagement and stay home and take a lukewarm bath to relax my nerves—which do you think I should do, Anna?

ANNA: I guess you'd better decide for yourself, Mrs. Fenway.

MRS. FENWAY: I can't decide! I've still got a headache. I guess it's from worrying so much about that boy. He's never given me trouble but he's been such a stranger to me, Anna, I never know what he is thinking.

ANNA: I think he's sort of shy, Mrs. Fenway.

MRS. FENWAY: Shy, yes, terribly shy. Where are my Camels? [*Lights cigarette.*] He doesn't like his schoolmates. Never did. And now his father wants him to stop school and go into the wholesale business, but I don't think that Donald would be a success in the wholesale business. What do you think of it, Anna?

ANNA [*pause*]: No. I guess he wouldn't, Mrs. Fenway. I guess Donald would be kind of lost in the wholesale business.

MRS. FENWAY: Yes, lost. That's it. Completely lost in the wholesale business. [*Pause.*] I think he should go in for some kind of creative work like his father but the trouble is that the poor boy doesn't seem to have any particular talent. Do you see that he's got a talent for anything, Anna?

ANNA: No, ma'am.

MRS. FENWAY: He likes to hear his father play but he never cared to study music himself. And his grades at school are very mediocre, you know. It's really quite a problem. The only thing he seems to care about is staying out here on the lake. All winter he talks about it and when spring comes he just seems to be living for the first of June when school closes and we come down here to the cottage and now the cottage is going to be sold and all and I just don't know—Anna, put this letter back up on the mantel, just the sight of that man's handwriting makes my head swim. I've been having black dots all day in front of my eyes. [*She leans back.*] I wish I could take an interest in mysticism or something like that. It seems to be so absorbing. Hasn't the *Saturday Evening Post* come out yet this week?

ANNA [*after a pause*]: No, ma'am.

[*There is a long pause in which we hear only the dull ticking of a clock.*]

MRS. FENWAY: Take that clock out of here. The sound of it gets on my nerves.

ANNA [*removing clock*]: Is that all, Ma'am?

MRS. FENWAY: No, you'd better phone the Vincents that I'll come after supper instead. I can't let my bridge go entirely. Look out the window and see if Donald's in swimming.

ANNA [*at window*]: Yes, Ma'am.

MRS. FENWAY [*sharply*]: He is or he isn't?

ANNA: Yes, ma'am.

MRS. FENWAY [*leaning back with eyes closed and one hand on her forehead*]: He's a strange boy. I never know what he is thinking about. He just looks at me with those sad far-away eyes of his—that remind me so much of his father's. [*She turns restlessly.*] I think he needs some young friends. I would send him to one of those special schools where they give individual attention or something if it wasn't just so expensive. He's growing up so. He'll be seventeen in September and still such a child.

ANNA [*after a pause*]: That's a funny age, Mrs. Fenway.

MRS. FENWAY [*sighing*]: Yes. Adolescence.

ANNA [*sitting down by the window with hands folded and a distant look in her eyes*]: They get so mixed up at that age. [*Pause.*] I remember I had funny ideas about things then. It was all very big and important and I thought that if I didn't get what I wanted the sun would stop coming up.

[*Pause. Anna blinks her eyes and remains motionless. A faint breeze stirs the gauzy white curtains.*]

MRS. FENWAY: Even the wind is hot this afternoon. And the lake is so glaring. I don't see how he stands it out there. Is he swimming?

ANNA [*turning slowly toward the open window*]: Yes, Ma'am.

MRS. FENWAY: He's just a dreamer. Like his father was. I flatter myself that I took some of that nonsense out of his father, though!

[*A long pause with clock ticking and Anna seated with hands folded and distant grey eyes.*]

MRS. FENWAY: What are you looking at?

ANNA: There's a gull flying over the lake. A white one.

MRS. FENWAY: I despise them! They sound like rats squeaking. Is Donald still swimming?

ANNA: Yes, he's swum out quite far. I can just see his head in the sun.

MRS. FENWAY [*turning fretfully*]: Yes, just a dreamer. Just like his father was before I got him to settle down. I never have quite understood people like that, Anna. They're like quicksilver. You can't put your fingers on them. Slippery. Senseless. There's no use trying to make them do like they should. —I hope Donald hasn't swum out very far.

ANNA: He's out pretty far.

MRS. FENWAY: Hasn't he turned back in yet?

ANNA: No, Ma'am, he's still swimming straight out.

MRS. FENWAY: He's a very good swimmer, though he was late in learning. At first he was afraid of the water, then all of a sudden he got so he loved it and ever since then the lake has been his main object in life. I think that's very odd of him, don't you, Anna? He doesn't seem to care for the companionship of other young people. I do so hope that he doesn't turn out to be just like his...

[*Her voice trails off and she turns on the other side. Again we hear the clock ticking.*]

MRS. FENWAY: I thought I told you to take the clock out. I can still hear it ticking.

ANNA: It's in the next room, Mrs. Fenway.

MRS. FENWAY: I guess I should have gone to play bridge.

ANNA: Yes, Ma'am.

MRS. FENWAY: Has Donald come in to shore yet?

ANNA: No, Ma'am, he's still swimming out.

MRS. FENWAY: Heavens! Still swimming out? [*She rises awkwardly and shuffles over to the window.*]

ANNA: Yes, Ma'am, he's still swimming out.

MRS. FENWAY: Heavens! Can you see him?

ANNA: Yes, Ma'am, that little dark spot's his head.

MRS. FENWAY: Anna! He's never swum out that far before!

ANNA: No, ma'am.

MRS. FENWAY: Where is he now? I can't see him!

ANNA: He's still swimming out.

MRS. FENWAY: Out?

ANNA: Yes, Ma'am, still further out.

MRS. FENWAY: Why doesn't he turn back in? Anna! Run down to the shore and call him back in. Quick, quick, before he— [*She thrusts her head out the window and screams.*] Donald!

[*There is a long pause. Anna slowly raises a hand to her throat. Mrs. Fenway staggers away from the window.*]

MRS. FENWAY: The sunlight blinds me. I can't see him anymore. Everything is black in front of my eyes. I can't see a thing. Where is he now? Has he turned back? [*A pause.*] I'm so faint. Light-headed. What's happened? [*She sinks into a wicker chair in the center of the room.*] Bring me a glass of water and my—my drops. [*Pause.*] Has Donald come back to shore yet?

[*Anna turns slowly away from the window and as she does so she crosses herself.*]

ANNA: No.

[*Pause.*]

MRS. FENWAY [*sharply*]: Why do you look at me like that?

[*Pause.*]

ANNA: No.

[*Pause.*]

MRS. FENWAY [*screaming*]: *Answer me!*

[*A long pause.*]

ANNA: No. He didn't come back.

CURTAIN

THE BIG GAME

(A ONE-ACT PLAY)

CHARACTERS

TONY ELSON, a college football star, age twenty
DAVE, a charity case, age twenty
WALTON, a middle-aged patient, age forty-nine
JOE, a hospital orderly
MISS ALBERS, a young nurse
FUSSY, nickname for MISS STUART, the head-nurse
DR. NORTH, a young staff doctor
DR. HYNES, Dave's physician

Scene: *A small men's ward in a city hospital. It contains at least three beds, only two of which are occupied as the play begins. The beds may be arranged in whatever order best suits the play's action, but Dave's bed must be so placed that he directly faces the windows. Tony's bed-table is heaped with a profusion of gifts, baskets of fruit, boxes or candy, books, magazines, flowers.*

It is early morning of a Saturday in Autumn. The dazzling white room is flooded with sunlight.

TONY [*noticing Dave is awake*]: Hello. You slept through breakfast. Know it?

DAVE [*listlessly*]: That's good. I'm glad they let me sleep.

TONY: Have another bad night?

DAVE: Awful. Seemed like I couldn't get my breath. Ten-thirty I rang for a shot. Didn't get it till nearly midnight.

TONY: I guess they don't want to give you too much of that stuff.

DAVE [*tensely*]: I *got* to have it. They *know* I got to have it. Why don't they *give* it to me when I ask for it?

TONY: They want you to get along without it as much as you can.

DAVE: Naw. They know I'm a charity case.

TONY: That isn't it, Dave. You know it isn't. They're really white around here.

DAVE [*after a pause*]: Didn't I keep you awake? I was afraid I would. I kept coughing all the time. Felt like I had a chest full of feathers.

TONY: Nothing keeps me awake. They ought to give you something to stop that cough, though.

DAVE: Oh, I guess they give me everything they could. What're you getting dressed for this early?

TONY: This is the day, kid.

DAVE: Oh. You're leaving, huh?

TONY: Hell, yes. If the Doc says it's okay. How does that leg look to you? [*He extends a partly bandaged limb.*]

DAVE: Still sort of swollen. But it looks a whole lot better.

TONY: I guess I'm damned lucky to have that leg.

DAVE: Yeah.

TONY: I came close to losing it. I'd rather be dead than go through life on a wooden leg!

DAVE: No, you wouldn't.

TONY: You don't know me, kid. I got to be moving. And moving fast. Damn! If they don't let me outa this place today— What do you think? You think they will?

DAVE: What makes you so anxious?

TONY: You dummy! This is *Saturday!*

DAVE: Oh, the football game.

TONY: The biggest one of the season. The one with Mizzou. Damn! If I miss seeing this game! Bad enough not being in the line-up! Just think! I only got to play in two games this season! Isn't that luck for you?

DAVE: Yeah. That's luck, isn't it?

TONY: Well, anyway I'll be sitting there on the bench this afternoon. You bet. Next game we'll have *you* out there, Dave. I'll have you sitting right down there on the bench with me.

DAVE: Yeah?

TONY: Sure thing. Lookit! Here comes Greta Garbo!

[*A tall blonde nurse, Miss Albers, enters the room.*]

MISS ALBERS [*with mock severity*]: What're you doing out of bed, Clark Gable?

TONY: I thought we oughta go through that big love scene again, sweetheart.

MISS ALBERS [*thrusting thermometer in his mouth*]: Wait till I see how hot you are this morning.

[*With a threatening grimace, Tony sinks on edge of his bed. The nurse goes over to Dave.*]

MISS ALBERS: I let you sleep through breakfast this morning, you little bum. I could've gotten fired for that if Fussy knew about it.

DAVE: Yeah. Thanks, Greta. I sure needed that sleep. They didn't give me a shot till nearly midnight.

MISS ALBERS: We'll give you one early this evening. [*She thrusts a thermometer in his mouth, counts his pulse. Her face is serious. She goes over to Tony. Removes his thermometer.*] Disgustingly normal.

TONY: That means I get out of here, huh?

MISS ALBERS: How could I bear to lose you, Mr. Gable!

TONY [*crouching and plunging toward her*]: This is how you make a line drive, Greta!

MISS ALBERS: Stop it, you nut!

TONY: Where's your interference? Where's your interference?

MISS ALBERS [*shrieking with laughter*]: Stop it, stop it, you fool! [*As Tony releases her*] I've already been accused of having too much sex appeal. They say it's bad for the old boys with the weak hearts.

TONY [*thoughtlessly*]: You better not start working on Dave when I get out.

MISS ALBERS: Dave doesn't like girls? Do you Dave?

[*She removes the thermometer from Dave's mouth.*]

DAVE: No. Especially not blonde ones.

MISS ALBERS: See? I haven't got a chance with Dave! Oh, God, here comes Fussy!

[*The voice of the head nurse is heard outside the door. Then she enters. She is a spectacled, middle-aged woman with sharp features. The younger nurse becomes very serious and busy.*]

FUSSY [*crisply*]: Good morning.

[*No one answers.*]

FUSSY: If I were you, Mr. Elson, I wouldn't be standing around on that leg. You don't know how close you came to losing it. And it's not all well yet. Those infections can't be fooled with. If I were your doctor I would suggest another full week in bed—but of course— [*She sniffs.*] I'm only a *nurse* around here! [*She turns to the younger nurse.*] We'll put him in this one. [*She points to one of the two unoccupied beds.*]

MISS ALBERS: Who?

FUSSY [*sharply*]: Didn't I tell you this morning we're putting that brain case in here?

MISS ALBERS: Brain case? No.

FUSSY: I didn't? Well, it just slipped my mind. No wonder. All the things I have to attend to *personally*. [*She turns back covers of empty bed.*] It's that brain case of Dr. Moser's. I never heard of not putting a brain case in a private room before but this one insists that he wants to be in with some others—he doesn't want to be by himself —temperamental!—so we'll have to put him in here, though Heaven knows—

MISS ALBERS: A brain case, Miss Stuart?

FUSSY: Surgical. Very delicate. Only Dr. Moser would attempt such a thing. Trying to remove a tumor from the left frontal lobe . . . .

[*As she is saying this with her back to the door, the new patient Walton, a middle-aged man, enters, followed by a staff doctor,*

Dr. North. They enter so quietly that Fussy does not immediately observe them. She is busy fussing with the bed.]

FUSSY [*continuing in a loud voice*]: I wouldn't give a *nickel* for his chances!

[*Dr. North quickly, sharply clears his throat. Fussy turns with a startled gesture. She gasps and raises one hand to her cheek—to make it all the more painfully obvious that the middle-aged man is the new patient whom she was talking about. His expression shows that he understood the import of her words. There is a moment of tense, strained silence.*]

FUSSY: Oh, I was just—just fixing his bed!

DR. NORTH [*coldly*]: Yes. Yes. [*Then heartily.*] Here you are, old fellow. This room is now called the "stadium." This is where we play our indoor football games every Saturday afternoon.

TONY [*cutting in*]: Not *this* afternoon, you won't! I'm getting *out!*

DR. NORTH: Are you? Well, we'll have to see about that!

[*Miss Albers, slipping behind Fussy, winks elaborately at Tony and slips out of the room.*]

DR. NORTH [*to the new patient*]: Mr. Walton, that young man over there's Tony Elson, All-American halfback on the Washington Bears! Tony, this is Mr. Walton, your new room-mate.

[*They shake hands. Walton's face is strained. All his movements are overcharged. Too quick. Tense. He is putting on a bold front.*]

WALTON: Glad to know you, Elson. I've seen you play. —What am I supposed to do? Go to bed? [*He laughs jerkily.*] Seems sort of ridiculous going to bed when I feel perfectly well!

DR. NORTH: You can undress behind this screen. Miss Stuart, you'd better take his history now.

[*A white screen is placed before Walton's bed. Fussy seats herself on other side of screen with pencil and notebook. Asks the usual hospital questions as Walton gets in bed.*]

DR. NORTH [*examining Tony's leg*]: Still a little swelling around the knee, huh?

TONY: It's okay.

DR. NORTH [*squeezing it slightly*]: Yeah?

TONY: Owww!

DR. NORTH [*smiling*]: I thought you said it was okay. Well, we'll see what Dr. Hynes has to say.

TONY: Be a sport, Doc. Tell him to let me out. I *got* to see that big game this afternoon.

FUSSY [*taking Walton's history*]: Date of birth?

WALTON [*huskily, from behind screen*]: December 3, 1887.

FUSSY: Parents living?

WALTON: No.

FUSSY: Age of parents at time of decease?

[*There is a silence. The young Doctor goes over to Dave's bedside. Dave has had his face turned away from the room, his eyes closed.*]

DR. NORTH: What're you so gloomy about this morning?

DAVE: I had another bad night.

DR. NORTH [*seriously*]: Sorry to hear that, fellow. [*He counts Dave's pulse.*]

WALTON: My mother died at the age of 52. My father was just my age when he died.

FUSSY: Cause of mother's death?

WALTON [*hoarsely*]: Cancer.

FUSSY: Of what organ?

DR. NORTH [*dropping Dave's wrist and putting away watch*]: What was the matter last night?

DAVE: They wouldn't give me my shot till nearly midnight. I kept coughing. Coughing. I don't cough during the day. Just at night. Feel like I can't breathe good. It keeps me awake. I wish they'd give me my shots when I ask for them.

FUSSY [*sharply*]: What organ, please?

WALTON [*angrily*]: Doctor, does she have to ask me all of those damn fool questions? I've got a headache now!

DR. NORTH [*quietly*]: That will do, Miss Stuart.

[*Fussy rises stiffly and departs.*]

DR. NORTH [*to Dave*]: Of course we have to give you the shots when we think they'll be most effective.

DAVE [*hysterically*]: I'm getting tired of it, Doc. It goes on night after night. I don't sleep. I just lie here looking up at the ceiling with that funny feeling inside me like I had a chest full of feathers!

DR. NORTH [*scribbling on pad*]: You've got to be patient, old boy. It takes a little time, that's all. We're going to take another snapshot this morning of your interior decorations. [*He rings bell for the nurse.*]

DAVE: X-ray? Them things don't do any good. I want something that'll *help* me. Something that'll give me some *sleep* at night.

DR. NORTH: We'll fix up a sedative for you tonight, Dave.

DAVE: Sedative's don't help neither. They don't make me stop coughing at night. I want to stop *coughing*. I want to get some *sleep*. I don't want to just *lie* here night after night looking up at the ceiling—and—and—*expecting*—

DR. NORTH: Expecting what?

DAVE: Nothing. [*He turns on his side.*] I'm sorry I made such a fuss. I didn't mean to.

DR. NORTH: That's all right, kid. We're all pulling for you, you know.

TONY [*who is now fully dressed*]: Sure thing, Dave. We'll have you up in time to see me play in that Thanksgiving game with the Blues.

DR. NORTH [*putting his instruments away*]: Dave's more likely to be watching that game than you are to be playing in it, halfback.

TONY: I'm going to be in the game and Dave's going to be on the bench watching me! How about it, Dave?

[*Pause.*]

DAVE: I never seen a real football game. Some kids in our neighborhood used to play Saturday afternoons in the corner lot. It looked like a swell game but it always ended up in a free-for-all fight.

TONY: Didn't you ever play, kid?

DAVE [*slowly*]: No, I never could play anything rougher than tiddly-winks. Whoever put me together sure made some awful mistakes. Whoever it was—I'd like to take a sock at the guy!

TONY [*laughing*]: That's the old fighting spirit, kid.

[*Miss Albers enters.*]

DR. NORTH: Get a chair in here for Dave. We're going to take another X-ray, Miss Albers.

MISS ALBERS: All right, Doctor.

WALTON [*from the bed*]: Say, Nurse, would you mind putting this screen away now? I've got a little too much privacy here.

[*She pushes the screen against the wall. Walton is now in pyjamas seated in bed.*]

WALTON: When does Dr. Moser get here?

DR. NORTH: About 1:30.

WALTON: He'll take me right away, won't he? I want to get this thing over with.

DR. NORTH: You're scheduled for 2:00, Mr. Walton. Impatient?

WALTON: Yes. The sooner it's over the better.

DR. NORTH: That's the way to look at it.

[*Intern enters with wheel chair. Dave is lifted into it.*]

DAVE: You've already got enough pictures of my insides to start a museum. They must be pretty remarkable looking. Lemme alone, please. I can get up. [*He stands and totters. They help him into chair. He grins weakly.*] Hah! Just like the boardwalk at Atlantic City! This is the life, boys!

[*They wheel him out of the ward.*]

WALTON: What's wrong with that boy?

DR. NORTH [*shaking his head as he makes some final notations*]: Congenital heart case. Damned rotten for a kid that age.

WALTON: Not much chance for him?

DR. NORTH: It's a question of time, that's all.

TONY: You mean he's— ?

DR. NORTH: I mean you're luckier than you think, Tony, just having to sit out a few football games!

TONY [*thoughtfully*]: I guess I am at that—*God*—I didn't know it was as bad as all that. Poor ole—*Dave!* [*He is temporarily sobered. Sits down on edge of bed to tie his shoestrings.*]

WALTON: I wonder if the kid knows it's that bad?

DR. NORTH: He's got guts. This is the first time I've ever known him to break down and make a fuss over it. Things like that— well—what can you do? [*He puts away his notebook.*] It's too damned bad, that's all!— [*Then heartily.*] So long, fellows.

TONY AND WALTON: So long.

[*Pause.*]

TONY: You see things in a hospital that make you think.

WALTON: Yeah. I guess you do—at that!

TONY: I never thought about things like that before. Of course I knew there were such things. People got incurable diseases and died. But I never saw them—happening!

WALTON: No, that's the hard thing. Seeing them happen. Not being able to stop it, either.

TONY: You wonder why a thing like that should happen to a kid like Dave. You can't figure it out.

WALTON: No. You can't figure it out—why a *lot* of things have to happen.

TONY: No, it doesn't make sense. It doesn't make sense, does it?

WALTON: No, it doesn't. [*Pause.*] It doesn't make sense.

TONY: It doesn't do to think about it much. If you think about it it makes you feel too funny—it kind of *scares* you, doesn't it?

WALTON: Yes. It scares you to think about things like that.

TONY: What are you in here for?

WALTON: Operation. They're going to— [*He taps his forehead.*] —take something out of my head.

TONY: Oh, yes. I heard.

WALTON [*in a strained tone*]: I heard, too. I heard what *she* was saying when I come in!

TONY: Oh—*that!*

WALTON: Yeah.

TONY: I wouldn't pay any attention to *that.*

WALTON: She wouldn't give a nickel for my chances! Huh! Maybe I'll fool her.

TONY: Aw, she's an old sour-puss—she wouldn't bet a nickel on the sun coming up tomorrow!

WALTON [*after a pause*]: These brain operations—they're ticklish.

TONY: My infection was ticklish, too—there was one night they thought they'd have to amputate!

WALTON: Gosh.

TONY: Yeah, I had fever. 105. Boy, I was raving! But still I had sense enough to tell 'em to let me die—before they cut my leg off! [*He grins.*] I guess ole Sour-puss was standin right there with the meat-cleaver—ready for action!—but I fooled her! [*He gets up.*] I'm going to be out there on the bench this afternoon just like I said I would. You bet your life I am! Coach is gonna spring some trick plays this afternoon'll make football hist'ry. We was working them out together last week. There's an end-play that's a honey. It's like this, see— Right tackle goes round— Naw —he blocks—that's it—he blocks and Joe Kramer– Hell! [*He snaps his fingers.*] It makes me feel sick at the stomach every time I think of it!

WALTON [*apathetically*]: What?

TONY: Me sitting on the bench! Imagine *that! Me* warming the *bench!* [*He grins.*] I guess I'm lucky at that. It's great to have a good pair of legs to walk on!— [*Sits again.*] That end play—oh, yeah—quarterback takes the ball—passes to Joe Kramer—Joe snaps it back to Chris Lange—you know him—he's taking my place in the line-up—Chris fakes a pass—then Joe . . .

[*At this moment Dave is wheeled back in by Joe, the orderly. Dave is very pale and weak-looking. He leans back in exhaustion but grins as he is pushed into the ward.*]

TONY [*heartily*]: Hi, there.

DAVE: Hi. I thought you'd be gone to the big game by now.

TONY: By Judas I oughta be!

JOE: Somebody to see you out there in the hall, Tony.

TONY: Doc Hynes? Hey, Doc—*Doc!*

[*He limps frantically out in the hall. We hear the Doctor's gruff remonstrances and indulgent laughter.*]

JOE [*helping Dave into bed*]: Easy does it.

DAVE: Aw, hell with it. Give me a lucky, Joe.

JOE [*reluctantly*]: Don't smoke it till after Hynes gets out.

DAVE: Thanks.

JOE: You ought to leave them things alone.

DAVE: The hell with it.

JOE [*seriously*]: You gotta take a little care of yourself, kid.

DAVE: What for?

WALTON: He's right, young feller. You don't want to do anything that'll interfere with your progress.

DAVE [*harshly*]: My progress! Nothing's going to interfere with *that!* Match, Joe. I'll save it till after lunch.

[*Tony hobbles violently in on a pair of new crutches, his face beaming. Behind him is Dr. Hynes.*]

TONY: I'm going, going, GONE!

DR. HYNES: Take it easy, half-back. Got everything?

TONY: Sure!

[*He slips into rest of his clothes, Dr. Hynes assisting.*]

DR. HYNES: Your Dad's got his car parked round the back entrance. It's closer. You've got to save all the steps you can, you know—don't you try walking anymore without those crutches for at least a week!

TONY [*impatiently*]: Okay, okay! Let's get going! I'll miss the whole first quarter! Most spectacular aerial attack ever witnessed! What time is it, Doc? Christ, that late? Oh— [*He turns back and goes to Dave's bedside, extending his hand heartily.*] So long, big shot!

DAVE: So long, Tony.

TONY [*a little embarrassed*]: Lissen—all these things—you know, the magazines and the candy and stuff—you keep 'em—they're yours!

DAVE: Oh, no. Them things was given to you, Tony. You better take 'em with you.

TONY [*grinning*]: Shut up! I don't want that sissy stuff! here— [*He places a large basket of fruit at Dave's side.*] You eat this stuff. I don't like it. *Honest!*

DAVE: I'll take a bunch of grapes, that's all. Thanks, Tony.

DR. HYNES [*outside*]: Step on it, halfback!

TONY [*going to the door*]: Coming! [*To Dave.*] You'll lissen in on the big game, won't you?

DAVE: You bet. I'll be listening.

TONY: So long. [*Exits.*]

DAVE [*as though to himself*]: Yeah. So long . . . .

WALTON [*after a pause, clearing his throat*]: That's a mighty fine young fellow.

DAVE: Yeah.

WALTON: I've seen him play football.

DAVE: Yeah?

WALTON: Best damned halfback the Bears have had in years.

DAVE: Yeah.

WALTON: I guess you and him got to be pretty good friends, huh?

DAVE: Yeah. [*Pause.*] Two months in here together. We got to be pretty good friends.

WALTON: You'll miss him, huh?

DAVE: Yeah. I'll miss him all right. [*He picks up a magazine, glances through it languidly, drops it.*] He made things lively in here. Always had something funny to say. You know. It makes you feel sort of less cut off from things having a guy like him around to talk to.

WALTON: Sure. I know what you mean. You and me, we'll have to organize a little pep-session all on our own! [*They both try to laugh—without much success. Walton keeps glancing nervously at his wrist watch.*] I've got about half an hour!

DAVE: Before they operate on you?

WALTON: Yes. They said it was best to get it done right away.

DAVE: I wish I had something they could operate on *me* for. Something they could cut out and patch up or something—instead of just—just . . .

WALTON [*after a pause*]: Brain surgery is ticklish business. [*He lights a cigarette. It trembles in his fingers.*] You heard what that old nurse said as I was coming in—she wouldn't give a *nickel* for my chances!

DAVE [*quickly*]: Aw, don't pay any attention to *her.*

WALTON [*excitedly*]: Wouldn't give a nickel for my chances, huh? I guess I'll show her something. I've been through tight spots before. I was in the war. I was at the front five months. Gone over the top in shell-fire. I'm not a-scared. [*He laughs shakily.*] Wouldn't give a nickel for my chances! [*His bravado fades and his face darkens.*] Still, I don't blame her. Brain surgery's a ticklish business. [*His voice softens and trembles a little.*] It's touch and go. That's what it is. Touch and go! [*He laughs again.*] I was pretty damned scared last night. Yeah. Just thinking about it. Lying there in bed trying to sleep. Couldn't sleep a wink. Kept thinking. Maybe this is your last night, old boy! The idea struck me funny. I couldn't get used to it. It's different when you're in the trenches. Then the shells popping all around you—things blowing up—big crash-boom-bang! —it gets in your blood and you go kind of crazy and almost forget to be scared!—but at night—alone—trying to sleep—and that idea in the back of your head all the time—maybe tonight's the night, old boy—no more nights after this one— Boy! It kind of gets to you!—when you've been yourself for forty-nine years—you know—you kind of get *used* to being yourself—and when you think of *not* being yourself anymore—of being *nothing* at *all*—just *dead!*—it kind of— [*He hastily lights a new cigarette.*] Know what I did last night? I got up and raised the window shade! I raised it as high as it would go! I raised it clean up to the top of the window!

DAVE [*with interest*]: What did you do that for?

WALTON [*huskily, after a slight pause*]: So that I could look at the stars!

DAVE: Yeah? Did that help?

WALTON: Sure. That always helps. When you're scared the best thing you can do's look up at the stars. That's another thing I learned in France. I remember coming out of a dugout one night after a heavy bombardment—I was scared stiff—walked like I was drunk—couldn't hardly hold my gun—all of a sudden I caught a glimpse of the sky—between the clouds of smoke—I laughed out loud—there was so damned many of them—stars up there—and there was only one of me—get the idea?

DAVE: Yeah, but what good does that do you?

WALTON: I don't know—it makes you feel kind of small and unimportant, they're so cold and far away—you look at them and say to yourself, well, what the hell do *I* matter? There's millions like me being born every day! D'you see? You look at those stars and you know they were there thousands of years before you ever came on this earth—and they'll be there thousands of years after you're gone! They kind of—represent—eternity or something! And when you think about a thing like eternity—when you think about a thing like that . . . . [*He makes a vague gesture with both hands.*]

DAVE [*slowly*]: Yeah—yeah . . . .

WALTON [*grinning*]: D'you see?

DAVE [*with slow comprehension*]: Yeah, I see what you mean ....

[*The lights fade out to indicate passage of time—about six hours. When the stage lightens it is evening. Walton's bed is empty, neatly made as it was before his entrance. Dave sits propped up. He is trying to read but his eyes keep wandering toward Walton's bed and Tony's old bed. He is obviously feeling pretty lonely.*

Joe, the orderly, comes in carrying a tray of food. His manner is hearty.]

JOE: Time to put on the feedbag, boy.

DAVE: I ain't hungry tonight.

JOE: You got to eat. Them's orders. [*He arranges the bed table, props Dave up a little higher.*] Spinach, kid. That's what you need. Lots of spinach. I told them to give you a double order!

DAVE: My pal! What's this goulash?

JOE: Lamb stew!

DAVE: I don't want it. Say. When are they gonna bring the new guy back?

JOE [*evasively*]: Who?

DAVE: You know! Walton! The guy who's having that operation.

JOE [*avoiding Dave's eyes*]: Oh. [*Pause.*] Don't worry about *that* guy. Eat your supper.

DAVE [*watching Joe tensely*]: He's been out since one-thirty. He oughta be through by now.

JOE: Yeah. [*Picks up magazine.*] He's through.

DAVE [*anxiously*]: Well, why don't they bring him back?

JOE [*after another long pause*]: That guy—he ain't coming back.

DAVE: You mean he—

JOE: Yeah. —Go on, eat your supper.

DAVE [*after a long pause*]: That's damn funny! He said he was comin' back. He felt pretty sure of it—from the way he talked.

JOE: Them brain operations—it's touch and go with them things.

DAVE: He knew it was—but he thought he'd make it.

JOE: Well, I guess thinking so didn't hurt him none. Eat your supper, kid.

DAVE: I ain't hungry. Give me a lucky, Joe.

JOE: Naw.

DAVE: Come on.

JOE: It's against orders.

DAVE: Come on!

JOE: Naw. You can't afford to smoke cigarettes. They're dangerous for you!

DAVE: You damn square-head! Give me a lucky! Come across!

JOE: By God if you ain't the stubbornest little whelp—Here! [*He extends his pack.*] Keep 'em, the whole pack! You can smoke yourself to hell 'sfar's I'm concerned!

DAVE [*taking them eagerly*]: Thanks!

JOE [*grumbling*]: You oughta quit smoking them weeds.

DAVE: Why?

JOE: You know they ain't good for you.

DAVE [*grinning bitterly*]: Nothing's good for me anymore, Joe.

JOE: Shut up. [*He gives Dave a light.*]

DAVE: What did you do with the guy after he died?

[*Joe doesn't like the question. Turns through a magazine.*]

DAVE: Take him down to that room in the basement?

JOE: Uh-huh.

DAVE: And then you cut the guts out of him, huh? [*He laughs faintly.*] What're you going to do with my guts, Joe? Feed 'em to that pooch of yours?

JOE [*violently*]: Shut up!

DAVE: You damn square head! I was kidding you, Joe. Say! How did that big game of Tony's turn out?

JOE [*rising*]: Bears won thirty-six to nothing.

DAVE: Thirty-six to nothing! Sort of one-sided wasn't it? That's the way it usually is—somebody wins—somebody loses—one side gets all the breaks! Well—I guess that made Tony feel pretty good!

JOE: Yeah, you bet. He had his heart set on seein' 'em win that big game.

DAVE: I guess they're celebrating right now—throwing a big party over at the Greek's.

JOE: The Greek's?

DAVE: Yeah, that's the place they go to celebrate. They drink beer. They get a little room to themselves in the back of the place—Tony says—and drink lots of beer. They get drunk and raise hell. Do all kinds of crazy things. Tony says there's a big redheaded waitress that's kind of sweet on him. She sits in his lap sometimes— [*He laughs slightly.*] Tony's the kind of guy the women would go for I guess.

JOE: Yeah, these football heroes—

DAVE: It ain't just that. He's got lots of life in him, Joe.

JOE: Yeah, I guess he has. Ain't you going to eat no more?

DAVE: No. Take the tray off my lap, Joe. And tell the cook I'm tired of this lousy slop—

[*He grins as Joe removes the tray. Then in a lower voice, moving fretfully.*]

DAVE: Joe, I think I'll take a shot of "dijjy" tonight—my breathing's kind of bad.

JOE: Want it right now?

DAVE: No. Let it go awhile. Just so I get some sleep.

JOE: I'll send her in about ten. Okay?

DAVE: Okay.

[*Joe starts out.*]

DAVE: Wait a minute, Joe. I wish you'd raise up that shade a little.

[*Joe raises the shade nearest him.*]

DAVE: No, the other one.

[*Dave points to one further over.*]

JOE [*with pretended annoyance*]: I swear you're gittin' fussier'n that ole maid in the East Wing. Is this the one?

DAVE: Yeah.

[*Joe jerks the shade up a foot.*]

DAVE: Raise it higher than that.

JOE: Higher?

DAVE: Yeah, higher!

JOE [*with elaborate care*]: How about this?

DAVE: Higher, Joe?

JOE: Oh! I get the idea! You wanta take a squint at that blonde upstairs—I get the idea! [*He raises the shade a few more inches.*] Is that okay?

DAVE [*impatiently*]: No. Higher. *Higher!* Raise it all the way up— [*Pause.*] —I wanta take a look at the *stars!*

JOE [*astonished*]: At the stars! Criminently! Is *that* all?

DAVE: Yeah. [*Pause.*] And you can forget about the shot of "dijjy"—I won't be needing it tonight!

JOE: *Sure* you won't?

DAVE: Absolutely certain. I won't be needing it— So long, Joe.

JOE [*as he goes out, quietly*]: Well—so long.

[*Joe closes the door behind him. After a moment Dave switches out the bed lamp. The ward is dark. We can hear him breathing very heavily. A match flares in the dark, lighting up his tense, strained features. There is an excited look in his eyes. He lights another cigarette. The glare of the match dies out. Dave leans forward. His hands are clenched. His face lifted. He is almost gasping for breath. He leans still further toward the window, drawing on the cigarette and looking up at the stars.*]

CURTAIN

THE PINK BEDROOM

The Pink Bedroom was first performed in Chicago, Illinois by The Dream Engine Theatre Company on January 19, 2007. It was directed by John Zajac; the set, costumes and lights were designed by Doug Valenta; the stage manager was Nazan Kayali; and the stage hand was Brent Collins. The cast, in order of appearance, was as follows:

MAN	Rob Biesenbach
WOMAN	Rebecca Prescott
YOUNG MAN	Troy Slavens

Scene: A pink bedroom. Everything is pink and fluffy with lots of little glass ornaments. A pretty blond woman of thirty in a pink negligee sits on the edge of the bed as a middle-aged man comes in. He grins at her tiredly.

MAN: Pink, pink, pink.

WOMAN: Yeah.

MAN: Everything's blushing in here. Blushing and blooming and waiting to be cuddled up. Well, well—

[*She stares at him coldly as he removes his overcoat.*]

WOMAN: Why don't you leave your overcoat in the hall?

MAN: I couldn't stand the postponement. I see you got the poinsettia.

WOMAN: Oh, yes—Yes, I—got the poinsettia.

MAN: Mommy no thanks?

WOMAN: Yeah, thanks.

MAN [*Sighs and takes off his coat*]: Don't mention it, Mommy.

WOMAN: No mention of New Year's?

MAN: Huh?

WOMAN: There's not to be any mention of New Year's Eve?

MAN: I thought we covered all that.

WOMAN: A party at home, you told me. A little party at home, for some Chicago buyers! Well— You must have a double in town.

MAN: How's that?

WOMAN: Some things I heard. Of a contradictory nature.

MAN: Yeh?

WOMAN: My friend Bess Sullivan went to the Elephant Room.

MAN: The what?

WOMAN: Oh, innocence, perfect! The Elephant Room at the Hotel Jefferson, yes, on New Year's Eve, while you were having that quiet little party at home with Chicago buyers! Your double was there, that secret twin brother of yours was entertaining a party of eight or ten couples.

MAN: What does it matter?

WOMAN: A lot.

MAN: Why does it?

WOMAN: You lied.

MAN: I couldn't avoid it.

WOMAN: Oh, you couldn't *avoid* it?

MAN: What else could I do?

WOMAN: Tell the truth.

MAN: And have you raise Cain here?

WOMAN: I never raise Cain.

MAN: No—just all of the time!

WOMAN: That's a lie!

MAN: Whatever I say you say lie!

WOMAN: *Only* when I have—

MAN: Go *way* out of your—

WOMAN: Absolute *proof* that you—

MAN: *Way* to—

WOMAN: *Lied!*

MAN: Oh, Helen, I'm tired.

WOMAN: *You're* tired. What about *me?*

MAN: You don't work from morn till midnight filling defense orders, Mommy.

WOMAN: How do you know what I do? I only serve one purpose in your life.

MAN: Now, now, Mommy.

WOMAN: Have you ever seen me by daylight?

MAN: You know that I spend every moment I can with my Mommy . . . .

WOMAN: I'll answer that question. No! You have never, never! And still you accuse me of—

MAN: Accuse you of—?

WOMAN: Idleness, wasting my time!

MAN: When did I—?

WOMAN: Just this moment.

MAN: You're picking a quarrel.

WOMAN: Because I ask for the truth? Go back to the Elephant Room at the Hotel Jefferson! —But don't send me no more scraggly plants and say you're with out of town buyers.

MAN: It's a fight—fight, fight!—between us all the time, lately . . . Honey, I'm not the champion of the world.

WOMAN: I'm not the challenger either.

MAN: You sure do put on the gloves every time I—

WOMAN: Stop right there!

MAN: I come in tired.

WOMAN: Yes, without phoning me even, at one o'clock in the morning!

MAN: It isn't possible always—

WOMAN: To stop in a telephone booth, to drop a nickel?

MAN: I thought I'd just slip in—

WOMAN: You think again! I ask—I *demand* the same respect as your *wife!*

MAN: How does respect enter in— ?

WOMAN: A ridiculous question!

MAN: Ridiculous, yes, that's how I would describe—

WOMAN: Just ask yourself this. Who made the sacrifices?

MAN: The moment that I come in— At once you bring up a dead issue!

WOMAN: Did I? Or did she? Which got the most and gave least?

MAN: What's that got to do with— ?

WOMAN: *Poinsettia!* [*Kicks the plant's pot.*] I'm to sit home with that poinsettia there while you—

MAN: I told you to take that twenty-five—

WOMAN: Did you suppose that I would?

MAN: —Dollar cheque and have yourself a good time!

WOMAN: Who with? With whom, may I ask?

MAN: You have—

WOMAN: *Girl*-friends, I suppose! But no—I don't—I have *nothing. Everything—all—given up!*

MAN: Don't *shout*.

WOMAN: I'll *whisper.*

MAN: Oh, God.

WOMAN: It's come to a show-down.

MAN: I come from one scene with my wife to another with—

WOMAN: Am I to be blamed that you hitched yourself up with a woman who's made a hell of your life?

MAN: First *here*—then *there!* and vice versa.

WOMAN: Because you can't—

MAN: Back! Forth! No rest for the weary, is there?

WOMAN: None! Till they make a decision!

MAN: What decision could I— ?

WOMAN: Just this! That I have as much of a claim as that brain-less society-chaser—your wife, and I—

MAN: You don't have to shriek abuse—

WOMAN: Oh! *I* shriek *abuse!* You should've been listening in on that telephone conversation—

MAN: That is another thing—

WOMAN: Yes! Another thing's right!—my phone talk with your wife! "What is your name?" "Never mind that," I told her. "Oh," she said, "you won't give your name. I don't blame you. Women like you are nameless in the sight of good people!" That's a direct quotation. "Women like you," she said, "are nameless—*nameless!*—in the sight of good people." I guess I should've been struck dumb but I wasn't. Oh, no, I managed to find a few choice expressions!

MAN: I bet you—

WOMAN: Yes, I found my tongue all right. "Why, you, clothes-horse," I told her— "A woman like you's not fit to—"

MAN [*clasping his head*]: *Oh!*

WOMAN: I laid her to filth I reckon! And when I was through she must've regretted she ever called me '*nameless.*' "Just what are your plans, your intentions?" "I have none," she said. "What are yours?" "I have none, either," I said, "but I *do* have some pride born in me, it seems like you *don't!*" "Oh," she said, "*pride,*" she said, "*have* you?" "I didn't *suppose*—" Yes! Pride! *Have* you! Sar*cas*tic!" Well—Shrieking abuse now, am I? You should have just cocked an ear at that Walgreen's telephone booth! Last Saturday morning! Right after the lovely poinsettia plant came dancing up to my door! Grimm & Gorly! Love from Popsy! Many Happy New Years! Oh, I found the occasion to use some choice expressions—they'll ring a long time in her ears before she calls me *nameless*!

MAN: The whole thing—awful, sickening, disgusting! My life has become a slop-bucket!

WOMAN: In which you jumped when you tied yourself to that—!

MAN: No! When I stepped out of line— !

WOMAN: Meaning me?

MAN: Yes, you, if the truth's what you want, meaning you!

WOMAN: What luck for you that God is hard of hearing!

MAN: I should've been—

WOMAN: If He could hear you, you'd be—

MAN: Satisfied with—

WOMAN: *Blasted* by—

MAN: Home—and—

WOMAN: *Lightning!*

[*They are talking at once, overlapping. She dashes a powder box to the floor. The man sinks exhaustedly on the bed.*]

MAN: —Children . . . This pink bedroom. Incurable disease. Worse than drink or drugs it has broken my will and made me a lump of flesh . . . An *obscene* lump of flesh!

[*He covers his head.*]

WOMAN: The scene is repeated. I might have known it would be. Again you become just—flesh as the result of a woman! Eight years ago it was her. Now I am the one that has murdered your beautiful spirit. The world is a circle and everything comes back to where it started. Yes, indeed. You came with your dissatisfactions to my front door.

MAN: Pink—pink—pink . . .

WOMAN: Oh, you've forgotten the state you were in at that time!

MAN: Everything—pink—pink—pink . . . .

WOMAN: So morbid you were, so neurotic—

MAN: The walls, the ceiling, the carpet—

WOMAN: You talked about *suicide* even!

MAN: Are pink—pink—pink.

WOMAN: Oh, how you *suffered* at home with that *self*-centered woman your—

MAN: Pink!

WOMAN: Wife!

MAN: Everything pink—the bed—the pillows—

WOMAN: My life then? Was complete! Headed I was? To success? *Straight!* Young.

MAN: Curtains pink! Lamp-shade pink!

WOMAN: Beginning to get featured parts at the Municipal Opera! Sat at home did I? Oh, no! I had no attention? Likely! Single men! Excellent prospects! More money in their pockets than you have in the bank! All to the winds! Yes! *Thrown!*
Out of pity. Your pitiful problems! Oh, what a heart-broken person who wept on my shoulders at night because no love, no comfort, no peace in his home! So tragic the life of this man, a fine mind threatened with break-down because of no love, no tender-

ness! Was I a *rock?* I was *not!* But a girl of nineteen intrigued by a grown man's problems. Love was your need and I gave it, not just an affair, but a real deep spiritual love. I gave it all of that time and still do *now* in spite of your *lies* and your—

MAN: —Pink.

WOMAN: Pushing me back in your life! If that wasn't marriage there's no such a thing as a marriage and what dogs do is the same as human beings!

MAN: Pink—pink—pink!

WOMAN: What are you muttering?

MAN: —Pink.

[*Pause. Clock ticks loudly.*]

WOMAN: —Pink?

MAN: Everything pink in this bedroom.

[*Pause.*]

WOMAN: Your idea, my darling. It was you that insisted that nothing but pink be included in this love-nest!

MAN: I had no conception how tired a man could become—

WOMAN: Or a woman either—

MAN: —Of just that one pink color. I'm forty years old.

WOMAN: You look it.

MAN: The time has past now in my life when—

WOMAN: Yes, yes, yes. So now you are ready to sing with the Methodist choir.

MAN: That's not what I mean. In the evenings we used to read books. Where is a book now? Or a good magazine?

[*Woman tosses a tiny volume from under bed.*]

WOMAN: The sonnets of Edna Millay. Please read one to me.

MAN: All of that part's finished. There's nothing left but the pink.

WOMAN: Get into your things. Here's your vest. Your polka-dot tie.

MAN: —What?

WOMAN: You better go home.

MAN: —Yes. [*Puts on the vest.*]

WOMAN: Your suspenders are dangling.

MAN: —Yes.

WOMAN: Your overcoat—here.

MAN: What am I getting dressed for?

WOMAN: You're going home.

MAN: No. I'm supposed to be in Chicago.

WOMAN: Then go to Chicago.

MAN: I can't go to—

WOMAN: Rent you a hotel room.

MAN: What for?

WOMAN: To sleep in. You're not sleeping here.

MAN: Why not?

WOMAN: It's pink. Please leave me the key.

MAN: Huh?

WOMAN: The front-door key, leave it here. Never mind, I've got it.

MAN: Helen—Helen—

WOMAN: Don't pity yourself. With the beautiful faith of the blind I gave you my life. Intelligent you who never let go of nothing! —*too smart to!* Goodbye. Go on, go on—Goodbye!

[*He turns around and goes out. She follows him. Slams the door. She comes back in. She calls out.*]

WOMAN: Arthur! —He's gone.

[*The opposite door is opened. A young man in red silk pyjamas steps out and grins at her. Pause.*]

WOMAN [*sobbing a little*]: What are you grinning at? Nothing's so terribly funny. I *did* love him *once* so *much* that I —!—really did . . .

[*The door-bell rings frenziedly.*]

WOMAN: —Turn out the light. —He'll go on ringing forever . . . .

SLOW CURTAIN

THE FAT MAN'S WIFE

The Fat Man's Wife was first performed at the Manhattan Theatre Club in New York City on November 11, 2004. It was directed by Michael Kahn; the set design was by James Noone; the costume design was by Catherine Zuber; the lighting design was by Traci Klainer; the sound design was by Scott Killian; and original music was composed by Adam Wernick. The cast, in order of appearance, was as follows:

JOE CARTWRIGHT	David Rasche
VERA CARTWRIGHT	Kathleen Chalfant
DENNIS MERRIWETHER	Robert Sella

Scene: An expensive New York apartment—early New Year's Day morning, 1938.

As the curtains open Vera and Joe are just returning from their New Year's festivities. It is immediately apparent that Joe has had the better time of the two. He is grinning fatuously to himself and seems a bit uncertain of his movements. He is a fat middle-aged man of the irrepressible type. Vera is also verging on middle-age but has kept her figure and her youthful grace. She reminds you— perhaps—of Lynne Fontaine. Enter Vera and Joe from New Year's Eve party.

JOE: Swell party!

VERA [*dropping her cloak*]: Yes, wasn't it, though!

JOE: I seem to detect a slight note of sarcasm.

VERA: Oh, no, not at all. It really was a lovely party. Obviously you were having the time of your life.

JOE: So was everybody else but you.

VERA: I'm sorry I was such a wet blanket.

JOE: That's exactly what you were. You just sat there all evening with your teeth in your mouth.

VERA: Isn't that the right place for one's teeth?

JOE: You might display them once in a while just to let people know you've got some.

VERA: Thanks for the suggestion. Next time I'll have them strung around my neck for everyone to gaze on with open admiration.

[*Joe starts for the cellaret.*]

VERA: Haven't you had enough to drink?

JOE: Not quite. It's New Year's, you know.

VERA: Yes, I'm beginning to suspect that it is. I'm going to bed. I have a splitting headache.

JOE: Sorry, dear.

VERA: Yes, I know that you are.

JOE: I'm getting one, too. I think I'll run around the corner for a bottle of aspirin.

VERA: There's a bottle of aspirin in the medicine-cabinet, but if you want to run around the corner—go right ahead.

JOE: Yes, I think the exercise would do me good.

VERA: No doubt it would.

JOE: I've been getting so fat lately.

VERA: Lately?

JOE: Another slight note of sarcasm, huh?

VERA: Oh, no, I was just reminiscing. You did have such a lovely figure when I married you, Josie.

JOE: I was always fat and you know it.

VERA: Were you? Well, I must have confused you with somebody else.

JOE: Possibly with young Merriwether.

VERA: Dennis Merriwether?

JOE: Yeah. You and he seemed to find a great deal in common tonight.

VERA: Oh, we did!

JOE: Talk about things being obvious, that certainly was. What were you and he doing in the Greenbaums' breakfast-room all that time?

VERA: We were simply escaping from the rather painful spectacle of you and that new Sarah Bernhardt of yours playing leapfrog with Mr. Greenbaum's dining-room chairs.

JOE: You and Merriwether must have been in there a couple of hours together.

VERA: Oh, did you notice? I hoped you'd be too preoccupied with Esmeralda Duncan to even miss me, Joe.

JOE: Esmeralda and I naturally had a lot of things to talk over about the new play.

VERA: Poor Dennis Merriwether! He said he'd never have written the play if he'd known it was doomed to be acted by that Esmeralda of yours!

JOE: That's gratitude for you! Merriwether's damned lucky to get an actress like Esmeralda to—

VERA: She belongs in a leg show!

JOE: Good legs are an asset in any kind of a show, for that matter, and if—

VERA: Dennis will think twice before he allows you to profane another one of his plays!

JOE: Allow me to—? Dennis—? Since when have you started calling him Dennis!

VERA: Since tonight!

JOE: Oh.

VERA: Don't be ridiculous. He's only a boy. Easily ten years younger than I.

JOE: I'm glad that you realize *that*.

VERA: Of course he's a very attractive one, too. In fact, he's the only person I met this evening that I would ever care to meet again.

JOE: Well, I'm afraid you won't have a chance to meet him again. He's sailing in the morning for the South Seas or something.

VERA: Yes, he told me.

JOE: Civilization is getting on his nerves. He wants solitude and the wide open spaces. Well, he's already got them, between his ears! —In a month or two he'll be flat broke and wiring us to send him money to get home on. I'll advise him to swim! Me produce another one of his plays? Never! I'm through with him. I had Greenbaum work in a swell bedroom scene in the second act. It would have clinched the show! Then Merriwether throws one of his artistic fits. Tears his hair all over the place and says we're crucifying the artist in him or something—the damned fool. Know what he did yesterday? Turned down a fifty thousand dollar bid from Goldmeyer Studios for that last year's flop of his! He wired Mr. Goldmeyer that Broadway had murdered the play and he didn't want Hollywood performing a post-mortem!

VERA [*smiling*]: Yes, that's like him.

JOE: Exactly like him! I suppose you think it was damned smart of him, do you?

VERA: No, I don't think it was smart of him. I think it was dreadfully foolish of him. But I'm glad he did it. It's nice to know that there are still some people that money can't buy.

JOE: Hmph! He's been lucky so far. The critics like his stuff. Right now he's their white-haired boy but in a few more seasons when they get tired of—

VERA: Oh, stop it, Joe! —Please unhook my dress for me.

JOE: Turn around then. —You could have knocked me over with a feather when that big hillbilly Merriwether walked into my office the first time. Here I was expecting an extremely polished, high-brow, cosmopolitan sort of person—naturally you would expect somebody like that from the kind of stuff that he writes—the first act in Vienna, the second in Paris, and the third somewhere east of Suez—and in walks a guy who looks like he just stepped out of a back-home cartoon!

VERA: He actually has been around a great deal. He was telling me about his travels tonight.

JOE: Yeah, in cattle-boats! There, it's unhooked.

VERA: Thank you, Josie. [*Vera goes into the bedroom.*]

JOE: What did I do with my door-key?

VERA [*from bedroom*]: You left it in the lock.

JOE: Did I? Why didn't you tell me so? Do you want us to be murdered in our beds some night?

[*Vera says nothing.*]

JOE: Well, do you?

VERA: Yes! I think it would solve all our problems very neatly.

JOE: Can't you think of any pleasanter solution?

VERA: Sometimes I wonder why I don't leave you, Josie. That would be a solution.

JOE [*blustering*]: Well, why don't you then? You've been threatening to for the last fifteen or twenty years!

VERA: There's always another morning. And you're so damned cheerful in the morning, Josie, that it's impossible for me to recapture the mood of the night before. I think if we ever get rid of each other it will have to be very abruptly some evening without our even saying goodbye—habit's such an overwhelming force! Have you gone yet, Josie?

JOE: I'm just going.

VERA: You haven't turned the light out.

JOE: I was just going to. Well—so long. —I won't be late.

VERA: Don't hurry on my account. And don't take too much aspirin, Josie—it's not good for you.

[*Joe struggles at door with obstinate key.*]

JOE: Don't worry about me—Vera, will you come out here and help me extract this goddam key from the lock? It always gets stuck! I've never known it to fail! [*Shakes door viciously.*]

VERA [*emerging from bedroom in negligee*]: Don't shake the door down. Here, darling. It's very simple. Here's your key. [*She deftly disengages key from the lock and hands it to Joe who pockets it with a truculent grunt.*] Not every woman would have done that for you, Josie. I'm sure Esmeralda wouldn't have been so obliging if she were in my position and I were in hers!

JOE: No? Esmeralda's a damn good sport!

VERA: Ah, yes. She understands you, Josie.

[*There is a musical bridge as Joe leaves, trotting briskly downstairs. Vera sighs slightly and goes over to the sofa; lights a cigarette, turns on the rose-shaded lamp and sinks down on the sofa in a reflective pose. Moments pass. Footsteps on stairs—a young man appears at the door which Vera has neglected to close.*]

DENNIS: Mrs. Cartwright.

VERA [*startled*]: Oh! You startled me out of a year's growth!

DENNIS: I'm sorry.

VERA: Oh, no, it's fortunate you woke me—heavens! My cigarette might have set the place on fire! [*rises*] But what a shame!

You just missed Josie! He stepped out a few moments ago—for a bottle of aspirin.

DENNIS [*removing his gloves*]: Yes. His bottle of aspirin has the most atrocious blonde hair!

VERA [*slightly disconcerted*]: Oh, yes—yes, I know. —But how did *you*?

DENNIS: I heard him making a date with her in the library at Greenbaum's while you were getting your wraps. That's why I came here, I suppose. Otherwise I wouldn't have had the courage.

[*Puts gloves in top hat which he places on table by door.*]

VERA: Dennis! Dennis Merriwether!

DENNIS: Yes?

VERA: I hope you aren't attaching *too* much importance to that—that little bit of accidental osculation that occurred tonight in Mr. Greenbaum's breakfast room.

DENNIS: Accidental?

VERA: Why, yes. You didn't think it was deliberate did you?

DENNIS [*after a pause*]: No. I suppose not. If it had been deliberate it couldn't have meant so much to me. You know, it's the things we do impulsively that matter the most.

VERA: Not always, Dennis. Sometimes we do things impulsively that don't matter at all, things that afterwards—we're bound to regret.

DENNIS: Do you regret it?

VERA: No. No, of course not. It wasn't important enough to regret.

DENNIS: It was important to me.

VERA [*pausing*]: I'm sorry. —Is that what you came here to tell me?

DENNIS: Not just that.

VERA: Oh. Something else?

DENNIS: A great deal! [*He goes toward her quickly.*]

VERA [*raising an arm to stop him*]: Dennis! —Dennis. [*Then more lightly.*] Hadn't you better close the front door? After all I'm in a negligee and you're much too young and slender to be mistaken for Josie. It's 1938! The beginning of a brand new year! But alas! I'm not so foolishly optimistic as to suppose it marks the end of evil-mindedness in all of our neighbors!

DENNIS: I thought the only advantage of living in one of these vertical places is that one doesn't have neighbors.

VERA: Yes, but you see there are elevators and the elevators have transparent doors.

DENNIS: I can't imagine that either you or I care very much about the good opinion of people coming up and down in elevators.

VERA: Perhaps I'm not quite such a free soul as you give me credit for being. There now, the door is closed. Please sit down.

DENNIS: You think it's terribly odd of me to come here?

VERA: No. I think it's nice of you to tell me goodbye before sailing. —You *are* sailing in the morning, aren't you?

DENNIS: I'm sailing in just three hours. But I didn't come here to tell you goodbye.

VERA [*lightly*]: No, of course not—just *au revoir!*

DENNIS: Not even *au revoir.* I came to tell you—hello!

VERA: Hello?

DENNIS: Yes. It's going to be a sort of continuous hello between you and me for the rest of our lives.

VERA: Now I'm beginning to understand! You're one of those remarkable persons that can be drunk as hoot-owls without looking like they've touched a drop!

DENNIS: Stop fencing with me—we haven't got time for that! You know very well that I'm perfectly serious and perfectly sober.

VERA: You don't talk like it.

DENNIS: Vera! Have you got such a tremendous respect for conventions?

VERA: No, I haven't got the slightest respect for conventions.

DENNIS: I didn't think that you did. So why do you have to behave like a silly conventional little ingénue when I make the perfectly sensible proposal that you and I chuck all this and go off someplace together where we can be our real selves!

VERA: Excuse me! I guess I *am* acting like a silly conventional little ingénue—as a matter of fact, I'm rather breathless!

DENNIS: I'll open a window for you.

VERA: Please do.

DENNIS [*at the window*]: There. —The snow's still falling.

VERA: Yes, I can hear it.

DENNIS: It makes a swell sound.

VERA: It sounds like cat's feet walking on velvet.

DENNIS: Listen! The bells are ringing again!

[*Bells ring.*]

VERA: Yes, I can hear them, too.

DENNIS [*turning toward her*]: They were ringing the last time.

VERA: What last time do you mean?

DENNIS [*approaching her quickly*]: The last time I kissed you!

VERA: Dennis! Did you notice, too? I think it must have been the sudden ringing of bells all over town that made it seem such an important kiss.

DENNIS: Was it only the bells?

VERA: I think it was only the bells.

DENNIS: No, you don't. You know better than that.

VERA: I thought that *you* knew better.

DENNIS: Are you really so cold as you're acting? I had an idea that you could be very warm and kind.

VERA [*pausing*]: I am.

DENNIS: Yes, I know that you are, Vera. I can feel your warmth all the way across the room. —Perhaps if I came closer I could feel it more distinctly.

VERA: No!—Sometimes propinquity has a chilling effect.

DENNIS: Not for us! It never could!

VERA: How do you know?

DENNIS: We belong as close together as we can possibly get. [*He goes to her.*]

VERA: Please!

DENNIS: I don't understand. I could have sworn you felt the same need that I do.

VERA: Please, Dennis! Go over to the cellaret and mix us a couple of drinks. Will you?

DENNIS: We haven't time. We can drink other nights. Tonight we've got too much to do. We're sailing in three hours, you know. Less than that!

VERA: Are we? I'm afraid it's too late to have it announced in the social columns. Our friends won't even have time to send us the usual slightly spoiled fruit and over-blown flowers.

DENNIS: No. Nobody will know that we're going until we've gone. We'll move out at daybreak. You'll see that faint pearly light over the harbor and the chugs and the wharves slipping by us like dark figures of a dream. The Statue of Liberty's huge, impassive dignity that you've mocked a thousand times daily in every act of your life you'll suddenly recognize as something beautiful and real and true. You'll see the western towers recede until they're lost in the fog. And then you'll sleep. And when you wake up the air will be washed clean. There won't be a sign of land left. Just a great wilderness of restless blue all around you and the wind in your face and the long white circles of gulls—

VERA: You make it sound very lovely and convincing. However I'd still like a taste of brandy.

DENNIS [*going to cellaret*]: All right if you insist on stalling!

VERA: What do you mean by stalling?

DENNIS: You know that we *are* going away together!

VERA: Please stop being foolish.

DENNIS: I knew that you were almost the first moment I saw you. Vera, I stopped being lonely that moment. I knew that I never would be again.

VERA: You—lonely?

DENNIS: Of course. Terribly.

VERA: But you've had such a full life.

DENNIS: Full of work. Now for the first time I can afford to stop for a while and pay some attention to my other needs and desires. Vera, you've been lonely too. Don't tell me you haven't been lonely, living here with that—that animated sofa-pillow that you call your—Josie!

VERA: Don't!

DENNIS: You've been so lonely that your heart's been broken a thousand times daily. Hasn't it? Hasn't it, Vera? Hasn't it? You aren't satisfied with the ordinary little acts of living any more than I am—you want something more the same as I do! You've been lonely, Vera, terribly lonely!

VERA [*taking her drink*]: Yes. I've been lonely. I think we're all of us more or less lonely. There isn't any help for it.

DENNIS: There *is!* We could have each other.

VERA: You're a boy. —I'm a middle-aged woman.

DENNIS: You could *never* be middle-aged!

VERA: That's the kindest remark any man ever made to a woman, and the most untrue! —How old are you, Dennis?

DENNIS: —Almost—thirty.

VERA: I'm over—forty.

DENNIS: You never were lovelier than you are now, Vera, and you'll never change.

VERA: Thanks. —I'll always remember you kindly for telling me that. —Hadn't you better be going now?

DENNIS: As soon as you're ready we'll go. Don't bother to pack anything. We can buy you a complete new wardrobe at our first port of call.

VERA: What port is that?

DENNIS: Acapulco.

VERA: Too bad. Too bad. I can't stand those bright tropical colors. They make my skin look sallow.

DENNIS: Be serious, Vera. We've less than three hours.

VERA: What kind of a boat is it, Dennis?

DENNIS: It's called a tramp steamer.

VERA: How lovely that sounds!

DENNIS: I knew you'd like it better than one of those luxury liners!

VERA: Oh, infinitely, infinitely better! [*She laughs.*] Excuse me for dreaming!

DENNIS: It isn't dreaming, Vera. I know the Captain. I've worked for him. I'll get him to teach you navigation. You'll learn how to steer by the stars!

VERA: Steer by the stars? How charming that sounds! But I'm afraid you'll have to tell the captain of your tramp steamer that my stars—are located in a different part of the sky—from those that he's accustomed to steering by.

DENNIS: That isn't so!

VERA: I wish it weren't so. But the facts are inevitable. [*Faces him.*] Now run along and be good! Next New Year's perhaps you'll be back in New York and we'll meet again at the Greenbaums' or somebody else's, and we'll have a long heart to heart talk in the breakfast-room while Josie plays leap-frog with the dining-room chairs or makes a pass at another blonde leading-lady—and when the bells start ringing all over town I'll let you kiss me again if you want to and then Josie and I will come home and presently he'll go out for a bottle of aspirin and you'll drop in to tell me goodbye again before you go sailing— That's the way our lives have been arranged for us, Dennis, and there's nothing intelligent that either of us can do about it! So run along now and be good and send me a picture post-card from Acapulco, preferably one of the native children—I love them—and tell me you're having marvelous weather and you wish I were there. Put an "X" in the corner if you wish—Josie will think it was just a pen-scratch!

DENNIS: Vera!

VERA: Yes, Dennis?

DENNIS: You know that we *would* have a marvelous time together.

VERA: Would we? What would we do?

DENNIS: So much! We'd swim and lie a great deal in the sun. We wouldn't talk much. There wouldn't be any necessity for it the way there is here. We could spend a lot of time just being—aware of each other—the way that we were when we heard the bells ringing tonight.

VERA: But aren't you afraid that in that tropical glare you might begin to see little wrinkles around my eyes which you hadn't noticed before?

DENNIS: If I did they'd only make you seem that much more beautiful and perfect!

VERA [*laughing*]: I think you're terribly nice but out of your senses.

DENNIS: Vera, your husband is fat. Not just physically fat. But mentally. He's mentally fat and—and I heard a woman at the party tonight asking some other woman who you were and the other woman laughs and said, "Oh, she's just the fat man's wife!"— It hurt me terribly to think that anybody should identify you—You, Vera!—as being simply the wife of the fat man who was making such a fool of himself at the party!

VERA [*with dignity*]: I'm grateful for your pity.

DENNIS: Oh, I know you don't want pity—I'm not giving you that. You know I'm not. You know what I'm offering you, Vera— a chance to live up to the best that's in you!

VERA: It's too late for that.

DENNIS: I'm offering you an open sky and an open sea and stars to steer your ship by!

VERA: That's too poetic to be very practical.

DENNIS: No, I'm not offering you a sixteenth-story apartment with Persian carpets and modernistic murals and a cellaret! I'm not offering you things like that. I'm offering you your chance to be really alive for a change. Won't you take it?

VERA [*after a long pause*]: Thank you, Dennis. It really is a splendid offer.

DENNIS: You *will* take it!

VERA: I can't.

DENNIS: You've got to.

VERA: Don't you see? It wouldn't be fair.

DENNIS: To Josie, you mean?

VERA: I mean, to you. It would be taking an unfair advantage of you. Oh, I won't deny that I'm tempted. What middle-aged woman known as the "fat man's wife" wouldn't be tempted by such an offer from such a personable young man? But it wouldn't be fair to take it. You've had a little too much to drink. You've had a great deal of success all at once. You've come to New York for the first time and met a lot of strange people with strange ways. It's gone to your head. It's made you a little bit dizzy. You hardly know what you're doing or saying, Dennis.

[*He starts to interrupt.*]

VERA: No, no, you don't. I can tell. You need fresh air and time to think things over. A few days out on the sea and you'll look back at this and it will seem—incredible. You'll thank your lucky stars that you got out of what might have been a very serious entanglement with a woman who is old enough to be—well, I won't say your mother, but at least your mother's youngest sister—You've never really been in love, have you? No, you've been too busy. Too poor. You've met women here and there in your ramblings that you've had a good time with. Drunk with and petted. And then forgotten. Maybe I'm the first that wasn't exactly that kind. The first woman you've met who could talk your own language. And it was New Year's Eve and on New Year's Eve everything is a little unreal. People say and do things they'd never dream of saying or doing any other time of the year. And I seemed attractive to you. Far more attractive than I really am. And you thought you wanted me. And if I were a little more foolish than I am I'd let you make that mistake. But I'm not going to, Dennis— I'm going to send you away.

DENNIS [*trying to interrupt*]: Vera, please listen—

VERA: Dennis, you'll find that there are lots of other women now that you have the time and the money. Flocks of them. Women almost everywhere. In all those thrilling places you're going. And most of them young and free—without fat husbands. So now—goodbye.

DENNIS: I won't go, Vera!

VERA: You'll have to go quickly—quickly!— That's Josie talking to the elevator boy. They must've been out of aspirin at the drug-store! —Dennis, go out the back way, please—there's another elevator at the end of the hall! [*She pushes him toward the rear door.*]

DENNIS: No, no, I'm not going without you! [*Catches her in his arms.*] You've got to go with me!

VERA [*kissing him*]: Goodbye, Dennis—you've been terribly nice!

DENNIS: You're going with me.

VERA: Hurry, Dennis!

DENNIS: You've got to make your decision.

VERA: I've made it. Goodbye. Goodbye!

DENNIS: No! I never sneak out the back way from any situation.

VERA: I see—the dignity of youth! [*She goes to the front door.*] Well, fortunately Josie isn't the melodramatic type.

[*She opens the door, admitting Joe who is still rather drunk and bewildered. He registers a dull surprise upon seeing Dennis. Vera is completely poised.*]

VERA [*taking Joe's hat*]: You came almost too late, Josie. Dennis dropped in to tell you goodbye before sailing.

JOE [*stupidly*]: Goodbye, eh? Oh, yes, goodbye, Merriwether— bon voyage and all that!

DENNIS [*with a wry smile*]: Thanks. [*Turns to Vera.*] And you, Mrs. Cartwright—do you wish me bon voyage, too?

VERA: I do—and with all my heart.

[*He faces her for a long pause.*]

DENNIS: Goodbye.

[*Dennis goes out. Vera closes the door.*]

JOE [*grumbling*]: The damn young fool—coming around here at such an hour as this—to tell us goodbye!

VERA: I thought it was rather sweet of him to bother.

JOE: Huh! [*Flops down on sofa with legs apart*] God but I'm tired!

VERA: Are you? —Did you get your bottle of aspirin?

JOE: Aspirin? What the hell are you talking about? Oh, *aspirin!* Oh, oh, yes, yes, of course—no—that is—er—the drug-store was closed—[*He groans abysmally.*]

VERA: Oh, was it? How dreadful—I'm so sorry!

JOE [*yawning*]: Yes, you would be.

VERA: Shall I help you off with your shoes?

JOE: Please, do, Vera. It's hard for me to stoop over these days. [*Slaps his abdomen.*] I'm getting so dreadfully fat. It's an affliction, Vera, to be so fat.

VERA [*sighing*]: Yes, I suppose it is—we'll have to bear it together. [*She rises and goes to the window.*]

JOE: What?

VERA: Nothing. Did I say something?

JOE [*sleepily*]: I thought you did.

[*Vera closes window and goes to bedroom door.*]

VERA: Well, if I did I'm sure it couldn't have been of the slightest importance. We'll have to get used to that, Josie.

JOE [*yawning prodigiously as he unwinds his silk scarf*]: Get used to WHAT?

VERA [*turning toward him at door and facing him with a smile that is not excessively cheerful*]: Saying unimportant things to each other for the rest of our lives!!

[*She leaves to the bedroom and slams the door shut. Joe looks up, startled by this unusual vehemence, and raises his eyebrows in momentary puzzlement. Then he yawns again and relaxes as the lights grow dim.*]

CURTAIN

THANK YOU, KIND SPIRIT

Thank You, Kind Spirit was first performed at the Tennessee Williams/New Orleans Literary Festival on March 17, 2005. It was directed by Perry Martin; the set design was by Chad Talkington; the costume design was by Trish McLain; the lighting design was by David Guidry. The cast, in order of appearance, was as follows*:

MOTHER DUCLOS, a spiritualist	Troi Bechet
YOUTH, seventeen years of age	Kevin Songy
WOMAN IN REAR	Janet Shea
FIRST YOUNG WOMAN	Buffie Rogers
SECOND YOUNG WOMAN	Stacy-Marie McFarland
MIDDLE-AGED WOMAN	Beth LaBarbera
YOUNG MAN	Jesse O'Neil
LITTLE GIRL, eight years of age	Katherine Raymond
FATHER BORDELON, a priest	Andy English
MR. REGIS VICARRO	Jonathan Padgett
MRS. DUVENET	Elizabeth Perez
MRS. VENINGA	Veronica Russell
OTHERS IN ATTENDANCE:	Angelina Gremillion
	Jamal Dennis
	Lucas Harms
	Rhonda Raymond

There can be one or more additional attendees, if desired

Scene: A little crib-like room on the far end of Chartres Street in the Vieux Carré of New Orleans has been converted into the chapel of a spiritualist. There is an improvised altar with multitudes of prayer-candles in little pearly white, pink, and green glasses. One whole wall is covered with religious pictures in rich colors. Innumerable little crosses and plaster saints are stuck about the room. There are bunches of artificial roses and lilies. The room swims with richly soft religious light and color.

The spiritualist is Mother DuClos, a small grizzled woman with a hunched back, robed in white like an angel. A little white, frilled cap is on her head. She is an octoroon and speaks with a Creole accent in a soft, emotional tone.

It is raining outside, a slow Autumn rain, and the wind is complaining a little. On the five crude benches are seated perhaps a dozen people, ranging in age from a little girl of eight to an old man of eighty.

On the rear bench a man and a woman sit rigidly apart from the others. The man is a priest but his clothes are concealed by a raincoat. The woman has a furious expression and keeps muttering under her breath as the service proceeds.

MOTHER DUCLOS: There seems to be an unkind presence somewhere. Somebody's come here tonight with evil thoughts in her heart and the thoughts are weighing heavily on the spirits. I see a dark black cloud like a thundercloud. —What's that, spirit?— Thank you, kind spirit. The spirit tells me that I should go right on with the service and just try not to notice the evil black cloud in the air. I see a boat. —Son, I see a boat. [*She is addressing a youth of seventeen.*] Does that mean anything to you?

YOUTH: Yes, Ma'am.

MOTHER DUCLOS: Are you thinking of taking a trip somewhere on a boat?

YOUTH: Yes, Ma'am.

MOTHER DUCLOS: Son, I wish that you would postpone that trip for a while. Put it off a while longer. You're going to find a good job right here in New Awleuns if you just keep hope an' faith. Don't go off on no long ocean voyage until the good Lord calls you.

YOUTH: Thank you, kind spirit.

WOMAN IN REAR [*in back—loud enough to be heard*]: She's just foolin' that boy. She's makin' all of that up.

MOTHER DUCLOS: Yes, there's an unkind presence, the spirits tell me there's an unkind presence but I should go right on an' just not take no notice. Annie. Annie. I seem to hear the name Annie. I see somebody on the other side of the river, tall an' thin with black an' grey mangled hair—name Annie. Does that mean anything to anyone here? Annie? Annie?

FIRST YOUNG WOMAN [*hesitantly*]: I had a grandmother name Annie but she was stout.

MOTHER DUCLOS: Honey, the spirits don't keep on all of their flesh. Time an' again I seen the spirits shed off their fat like a snake sheds off it skin on a barb-wire fence. Spirits are delicate things. They don't have all the gross desires of the flesh. Even their figures seem to change in appearance and get young an' slender again.

WOMAN IN REAR: Listen to that! Going on like that!

MOTHER DUCLOS: An unkind presence tonight, an unkind presence! What's that, please? —Thank you, kind spirit, I will. Yes, kind spirit! Yes! Annie says just sit tight an' everything's going to work out but you've got to keep patience. —What's that, Annie?

—Awww. Annie says don't hold a grudge against that neighbor-woman.

WOMAN IN REAR [*mockingly*]: Annie, Annie!

MOTHER DUCLOS: Annie says sticks and stones can break our bones but bad names never harm us! I feel something pressing in here. [*Touches her forehead.*] Honey, you've got to stop strainin' your eyes so much.

FIRST YOUNG WOMAN: Is that what gives me my headache?

MOTHER DUCLOS: That's what gives you your headaches. —See me after the service, I got somethin' fo' yuh.

FIRST YOUNG WOMAN [*resuming her chair*]: Thank you, kind spirit.

MOTHER DUCLOS: Now it appears that another young lady here is deeply troubled in heart because of a man.

[*Second young woman rises.*]

SECOND YOUNG WOMAN: Mother DuClos?

MOTHER DUCLOS: Yes, Sister?

SECOND YOUNG WOMAN [*huskily*]: I been quit by my husband.

MOTHER DUCLOS [*sadly*]: This young woman here says she's been quit by her husband. When did he quit you, Sister?

SECOND YOUNG WOMAN: Just about three weeks ago.

MOTHER DUCLOS: Just about three weeks ago. [*Tentatively.*] Seems to me like I can make out the shape of another figure . . .

147

SECOND YOUNG WOMAN: Is it a woman?

MOTHER DUCLOS: Yes, it's a female figure and kind of big in proportions.

SECOND YOUNG WOMAN: Blond-headed? Bleached? With glasses?

MOTHER DUCLOS: Yes, yes, yes! Thank you, spirit!

SECOND YOUNG WOMAN: That's her!

MOTHER DUCLOS: Full of deception, makin' all kinds of pretenses!

SECOND YOUNG WOMAN [*excitedly*]: That's her, that's the woman!

MOTHER DUCLOS: Posin' as decent but livin' in shame an' corruption!

WOMAN IN REAR: Describin' herself! She's givin' a perfeck description of her own self!

MOTHER DUCLOS: The spirits are troubled because of a loud disturbance on the back bench. Your husband is going to come back to you, Sister. Say your prayers, keep on sayin' your prayers, an' make a little sacrifice of money—

WOMAN IN REAR [*loudly*]: Don't you give her a cent, don't give her a penny for tellin' you all them lies!

MOTHER DUCLOS: A spirit behind me is whisperin' in my ear to keep on goin' an' not to pay no attention to this disturbance. Your husband is going to come home drunk on Christmas. —Maybe a little before Christmas, maybe a little bit after, but right near Christmas—

SECOND YOUNG WOMAN: That's how he left, he was drunk!

MOTHER DUCLOS: An' that's the way he'll come home! Rollin' home stinkin' drunk without a dime in his pocket!

SECOND YOUNG WOMAN: Won't he write me a letter when to expect him?

MOTHER DUCLOS: No, he won't write you no letter, don't be expectin' no letter, he'll just come rollin' home drunk an' flop on the bed an' turn that whiskery face with the bad-smellin' breath to th' wall.

SECOND YOUNG WOMAN [*laughing and crying*]: That's how he always used to come back to me!

MOTHER DUCLOS: Don't ask him no questions, don't even call him by name, just take off his shoes and take the dirty clothes off him and leave him alone on the bed to grunt an' snore an' talk in his sleep till mawnin'. Wash out his clothes, hang 'em outside to dry. When he gets up he's gonna be cold sober!

SECOND YOUNG WOMAN [*rapturously*]: Thank you, thank you, kind spirit!

MOTHER DUCLOS: As sweet an' fresh an' sober as when he was married. All that you gotta's do is keep on prayin' an' make a little sacrifice of money—

WOMAN IN REAR: That's right—money!

MOTHER DUCLOS: A dollar, half a dollar, anything you can spare to convince the spirits!

WOMAN IN REAR: Never forgets to mention the money, does she?

MOTHER DUCLOS: A terribly unkind presence on the back bench seems to be troubling the spirits. [*To a middle-aged woman.*] Sister, you want to ask something?

MIDDLE-AGED WOMAN [*rising*]: This awful weak, drugged-out feeling I have in my legs an' my back an' through my shoulders an' neck—Is it gonna wear off bye an' bye?

MOTHER DUCLOS: It's gonna wear off but it's gonna take *time* to wear off.

MIDDLE-AGED WOMAN: Well, ought I keep prayin' or ought I to go to the doctor? You see, it's like this, I don't make very much money—an'—

MOTHER DUCLOS [*producing a Coca-Cola bottle of water*]: Drink this wonderful Lady of Lourdes spring water—

[*Woman in rear laughs sharply.*]

MOTHER DUCLOS: Drink it faithfully, sprinkle it over your body, rub it into your skin! All it costs is twenty-five cents a bottle. What you've got, young lady, is *female* trouble. —That's what the spirits tell me . . . .

MIDDLE-AGED WOMAN: Thank you, kind spirit. [*She sits. Pause.*]

MOTHER DUCLOS: Now I'm seein' a big white piece of paper. It looks to me like an application blank. —Has anyone here filled out an application?

YOUNG MAN [*jumping up eagerly*]: That's me, Mother!

MOTHER DUCLOS: Thank you, thank you, kind spirit. It seems to me like a signature is needed.

YOUNG MAN: That's right, Mother!

MOTHER DUCLOS: Son, that paper is practickly signed already! Now I feel another person's affliction. This one seems to be a *little* person. What's that, spirit? A little afflicted girl?

[*In the far corner a little girl rises.*]

LITTLE GIRL [*breathlessly*]: Maybe that's—for *me?*

MOTHER DUCLOS: Yes, honey, bless you' heart! Come on out of that corner, let the little girl through, come on up to the front where the spirits can touch you! Now show Mother where it hurts, God bless yuh!

[*The child extends her arms and whispers something.*]

MOTHER DUCLOS: Awww!—Yes? —Ain't that a *shame!* The joints of this child's arms are swole up with bad bone trouble. There's rottenness in the bones that won't come out. She told me the doctors had operated and still the trouble come back. They call it a long, hard name and they say that it's hopeless. —That's what the doctors think. The spirits know better. The spirits tell me this child is going to get well, the bad bone trouble is going to be cleared away and the limbs are going to be pulled out straight again. Not by operations but just by faith.

LITTLE GIRL [*with hysterical joy*]: Thank you, thank you, kind spirit!

MOTHER DUCLOS: I want you to go to St. Roch's cemetery on Saturday afternoon. I want you to go alone with your beads and

I want you to make the journey around the stations, I want you to make all the stations and say your prayers and your beads. When you come to the third station you'll feel an icy cold chill, as cold as a winter's day, and the crooked limbs will be made straight again! Praise the Lord, be praised! Yes, thank you, thank you, kind spirit!

LITTLE GIRL: Thank you, thank you, kind spirit!

WOMAN IN REAR [*rising suddenly*]: Stop! Stop this right now!

[*The people on the benches turn to face her. Mother DuClos marches with slow dignity down from the altar.*]

MOTHER DUCLOS: An unkind presence is manifestin' itself! What have you come here for, sister?

WOMAN IN REAR: I come here to expose you, you old Voodoo nigger, you!

[*Mother DuClos stiffens visibly and sways.*]

WOMAN IN REAR: Yes, nigger—nigger! Call yourself Creole, dontcha? —That's just one of her lies! Lookit that kinky wool on 'er, an' lookit them thick nigger lips! Just an ole Voodoo nigger puttin' on make-believe spirits an' in the name of Jesus, too! You don't *see* no spirits, you don't *hear* no spirits, all of that's made up to fool these here poor people. It ain't even imagination, it's just plain old ordinary *lyin'*!

MOTHER DUCLOS [*trembling*]: Help me, kind spirit, against this evil woman.

WOMAN IN REAR: I won't even mention all the lies you sprung on me one time. Told me a very dear cousin of mine was gonna recover from a bad illness. Died the very next week of intestinal cancer! Told another good friend she seen a middle-aged lawyer and lots of money was gonna be passed around. Why, that poor woman, her husband passed away and never left her even money enough to pay for the coffin!

[*The crowd murmurs and stirs. One woman gets up and leaves.*]

MOTHER DUCLOS: Forgive this woman, kind spirit, have mercy upon her soul! [*She retreats a few steps toward the altar.*]

WOMAN IN REAR: You might as well quit that mumbling, I've got the goods on you this time. This here is Father Bordelon from St. Theresa's Parish. He'll back me up in everything I say. He knows what a faker she is, what a cheat and a liar she is! That water she says is Lady of Lourdes spring water—her nextdoor neighbors have seen her fillin' the bottles with it right at the kitchen sink! —Right from the faucet in her filthy ole kitchen!

[*Louder murmuring. Several of the group stand up and stare indignantly at the spiritualist.*]

WOMAN IN REAR: Why, I'd be afraid to put my lips to that "miraculous" water! What does she do with her money she gets from you people? She spends it on *liquor! Honest!* She spends it on dago *red wine!* Mr. Regis Vicarro, right over there by the door, is my witness on that! Every weekend, he tells me, she comes in his store an' buys her a gallon jug of that dago red wine! Religious purposes, she tells him! What kind of religious purposes would that *be,* I wonder? Furthermore she comes back sometimes in the *middle* of the week to buy *more*— Come in drunk with the smell of it on her breath to buy some more! —Promises, promises, promises! —Never *pays!* I wish you would take a look in the back of her house. Go on back there and see! What a disgraceful mess!

She lives in filth like a pig and comes out front all dressed in white like an angel! Had three children and all of them went to the dogs. Two sons in the penitentiary and her daughter's a common street-walker! What kind of spirits would have anything to do with a creature like that? How does she dare to say that you folks' precious departed would come in here and *talk* to her? Why, they wouldn't even *spit* on her, that's how low she is, common ole Voodoo *nigger!*

[*Two women start out the door.*]

WOMAN IN REAR: No! Wait! Don't go! —I've got a job for you ladies! Father Bordelon wants you to take out all of these sacred pictures and images she's stuck up! Tear them down from the walls and take them away! They don't belong in this place, it's *blasphemous* for her to have such things around here! You, Mrs. Duvenet, take that Virgin out with you! Mrs. Veninga, take that one of Saint Agnes! Blow out those holy candles, blow out *all* of them candles!

[*Crowd ad-libs excitedly—the young man laughs and blows out candles.*]

WOMAN IN REAR: That's right, don't leave a one a them holy candles burning, blow them all out, all out! Leave the old witch in darkness like she belongs! Cheater! Liar! Devil!

[*The group, with gathering violence, begins to remove the religious articles from the room. Stunned and speechless, Mother DuClos shrinks against the altar.*]

WOMAN IN REAR [*advancing on her*]: Get out of the way! I'm going to take out that statue!

MOTHER DUCLOS: Leave me my Jesus!

WOMAN IN REAR: You ain't fit to *look* at him.

MOTHER DUCLOS: Leave me my precious Jesus! Please, please, please, kind spirit!

[*The woman grabs her wrist and pulls her roughly away. Embraces the large plaster Christ and hands him to the priest who bears him outside. Now the walls are stripped bare of the colored pictures, the candles are all blown out, the room is nearly in darkness. The shuttered doors are pushed open and the angry crowd goes out. Mother DuClos is left alone in her pillaged chapel. —A solitary, guttering candle remains. —She retreats toward this, mumbling and wringing her hands. The shuttered doors bang open and closed in the wind and a gust of rain sweeps through them. The angry voices subside—a tamale vendor cries his wares in the distance.*

Out of a shadowy corner the child with the crooked arms shuffles awkwardly through the overturned benches and chairs and touches the old woman's shoulder.]

LITTLE GIRL: Mother—Mother DuClos!

[*The old woman stares at her blindly.*]

LITTLE GIRL: —*I* believe in the spirits! *I* still believe in the spirits!

[*Sobbing but tenderly smiling, the old woman gathers the child in the wing-like arms of her robe.*]

MOTHER DUCLOS: *Thank* you—*Thank* you, kind spirit!

SLOW CURTAIN

THE MUNICIPAL ABATTOIR

The Municipal Abattoir was first performed by the Shakespeare Theatre on April 22, 2004 at the Kennedy Center in Washington D.C. It was directed by Michael Kahn; the set design was by Andrew Jackness; the costume design was by Catherine Zuber; the lighting design was by Howell Binkley; the sound design was by Martin Desjardins; and original music was composed by Adam Wernick. The cast, in order of appearance, was as follows:

BOY	Cameron Folmar
GIRL	Carrie Specksgoor
CLERK	Thomas Jay Ryan

The pavement of a city street; the street itself is invisible. Behind the pavement is a wall of gray concrete over which are pasted poster-photographs of a military dictator, and at the bottom of the posters the word "Viva!" It is summer dusk. A boy and girl, university students, walk along the pavement, the girl crying, the boy carrying a furled flag. In the distance, the band music of a parade: it stays at a low level till near the end of the play.

GIRL [*as the boy stops*]: Is this where?

BOY: Yes. Go away now. You're making us conspicuous.

GIRL: Can't you stay back of the wall?

BOY: Of course not. I have to run into the street to make sure I don't miss. [*He gives her a quick, hard kiss.*] Now go away.

GIRL: It didn't have to be you!

BOY: Stop that!

GIRL: It could've been someone older, someone sick or ugly!

BOY [*stripping off his wrist watch and ring*]: Take these. Now go. There's a man looking at us. Cross through the park at the next corner. Go!

[*He kicks at her feet: she runs off, sobbing. After a moment or two a middle-aged clerk appears on the walk and stops by the student.*]

CLERK: Excuse me, young man.

BOY: What is it?

CLERK: Would you be, could you be, kind enough to direct me to the Municipal Abattoir?

BOY: —Did you say to the—?

CLERK: To the Municipal Abattoir. I seem to have lost the slip of paper I'd written the address on, and I'm already late.

BOY: —You work at the Abattoir?

CLERK: Oh, no, oh, no, I'm—I mean I was till yesterday a clerk in the Office of National Economy, but I was discharged and today I was condemned.

BOY: What were you condemned for? Do you know?

CLERK: There are several possible reasons. I did something foolish last week. I passed a tobacco shop and in the window of the shop was a wire contraption, a, a, a—treadmill, a wire cage that turned. It had a small animal in it, a squirrel, something like that, or a chipmunk, something like that, and it was running and running and running in the wire cage, the treadmill, and it looked—frightened, It looked panicky to me, so I was very foolish, I went in the shop and spoke to the proprietor about the little animal in the turning wire cage. I asked if the creature ever got out of the treadmill or had to keep running in it all the time and the man in the shop, the proprietor of the shop, flew into an awful rage over my questions, he caught hold of me by my coat and jerked my wallet out of my pocket and took down my name and address and place of employment and said he was going to have me condemned for interfering with something that wasn't my business. I think he must have done that since I've been ordered to the Municipal Abattoir. But there's another possible reason I've been sent there. When my daughter was drafted into the Municipal Whorehouse, I—I made, I wrote an appeal to the . . .

BOY: You received a written notice?

CLERK: No, no, just a phone . . . call.

BOY: It could be just a cruel joke someone's played on you. I think that's what it must be or they would have come to your place to put you under arrest and taken you to the Abattoir in a truck.

CLERK: They don't always do that now. Sometimes you're just instructed to be at the Abattoir at a certain time and you—go there. And I've been told they make it harder for you if you get there late, they don't get it over with quickly.

BOY: Do you have a dime in your pocket?

CLERK: No, I left all my money with my wife.

BOY: Here's a dime for you. There's a tram at the next cross street and you take that tram as far as it goes in either direction. Then you get off it and walk and keep walking.

CLERK: Surely that isn't the way to the Municipal Abattoir. I mean the Abattoir couldn't be in both directions.

BOY: Have you ever gone hunting? With a gun?

CLERK: Yes, during the meat shortage, my son and I went rabbit hunting.

BOY: Then you can use a gun, can you?

CLERK: Yes, I can, my son taught me.

BOY: Can you aim accurately? At close range?

CLERK: Why, yes, but—

BOY: I advise you to pull yourself together, respect yourself as a man, and go as far away from the Municipal Abattoir as you can go on the dime I gave you, and then—get lost.

CLERK: You're a young man, and you think that way because you haven't been a Municipal Employee for more years than you can count. As for me, when I'm told to do something by someone in authority, I do it without a question.

BOY: Your body cut and pulped by a mashing machine and sold in tins to be eaten by any Tom, Dick or Harry and their wives, children and dogs.

CLERK: Can't you see how terrified I am of it? I might have tried to protest, to appeal, but you see, when I was your age, I was a— *pacifist*! So, no, now I . . . see no possible way to avoid, to choose otherwise, since I really don't have any choice, and after all, being unemployed now and not wanted at home, I—

BOY: You have a family?

CLERK: Yes, a wife and—

BOY: How does your wife feel about you going to the Municipal Abattoir?

CLERK: Oh, she feels, as I do, that I have no choice in the matter.

BOY: A choice is something you have to invent for yourself, so go down to the next traffic light, wait for the tram and take it and stay on it as far as it goes. I've given you that free advice and I've given you your tram fare and there's nothing else I can give you or do for you.

CLERK: Yes, yes, I know, thank you, but you could possibly tell me where the Abattoir is.

BOY: That's right, I could, but I won't.

CLERK: You're the only person I know, if I may say that I know you, who doesn't think I should go there.

BOY: Hell, go there, go there, if you've lost the power to choose anything for yourself. But I'll tell you something. Hear the procession coming?

[*There is distant band music.*]

BOY: It's coming right by here and I'm going to interrupt it with this little instrument of interruption. Feel it in my pocket. [*He seizes the Clerk's hand and places it on his pocket.*]

CLERK: Is it—?

BOY: Yes, a revolver containing six bullets.

CLERK: No, no, no, throw it over the wall, They'll shoot you down if they—!

BOY: What a scared little man you are, and yet you asked me the way to the Municipal Abattoir.

CLERK: I do what I'm told to do, I go where I'm told to go, I never question instructions.

BOY: Good. I will give you instructions, I'm your commander, now. You are my slave.

CLERK: How am I your slave?

BOY: By appointment, just now. Look me in the eyes, straight in the eyes, and think of your daughter in the Municipal Whorehouse, used by diseased, dirty men. She'd cover her face if you ever saw her again because her skin would be covered with—

CLERK: DON'T, DON'T, DON'T!

BOY: Do what I tell you to do! Take this bloody flag in one hand, this revolver in the other and make sure the flag hides the revolver which is loaded for bear. Understand me?

CLERK: Yes, but—

BOY: You're going to do exactly as I say. You are my slave, I am your commander. Now, then. The procession is going to pass right by here in about a minute. The General's car is the first one behind the motorcycles. Understand me?

CLERK: Yes, but—

BOY: Just say yes. No buts.

CLERK: —Yes.

BOY: All right. When the first limousine is about to pass by here, you scream out "Viva, Viva!" and wave your flag, at the same time running into the street. And before you are stopped, you empty this revolver, loaded for bear, directly into the face and chest of the General, fast, fast, fast as you can. Okay, slave? Understand me?

CLERK: —Yes.

BOY: It will be quicker and easier for you than keeping your appointment at the Municipal Abattoir and your name and picture will be on the front page of every newspaper in the world. Understand me?

CLERK: —Yes.

BOY: Then I'll leave you here. But remember my eyes and the eyes of the whole world are on you. Accidentally, just through asking a question of someone unknown on a street, your meaningless life is elected to glory, and your death to the death of a hero. Goodbye. Embrace me [*He draws the man into his arms, then thrusts him back.*] Dear slave, immortal saint, martyr, and hero!

[*He leaves over the low wall back of the pavement. The procession comes roaring by.*]

CLERK [*waving banner*]: Viva, Viva, Viva, Viva, Viva, Viva, Viva!

[*The roar of the procession dies out.*]

CLERK [*to audience*]: I wonder if you would be kind enough to direct me to the Municipal Abattoir. I don't want to be late. They make it harder for you if you don't come on time . . . . Oh. I'll write it down. Thank you!

[*He removes a little notebook from a pocket and writes down the address as the stage dims out.*]

CURTAIN

ADAM AND EVE ON A FERRY

Adam and Eve on a Ferry was first performed at the Manhattan Theatre Club in New York City on November 11, 2004. It was directed by Michael Kahn; the set design was by James Noone; the costume design was by Catherine Zuber; the lighting design was by Traci Klainer; the sound design was by Scott Killian; and original music was composed by Adam Wernick. The cast, in order of appearance, was as follows:

D.H. LAWRENCE	David Rasche
FRIEDA LAWRENCE	Kathleen Chalfant
A VISITOR, ARIADNE PEABODY	Penny Fuller

Scene: The sun porch of a villa in the Alps Maritimes. There are numerous potted plants and on the back wall a kind of banner bearing the woven figure of a phoenix in a nest of flames, which happens to be the personal symbol of the red-bearded man seated in the reclining chair. He wears a gold satin dressing-robe with a lavender knitted shawl about his shoulders and he is doing some fine needle-work as the curtain rises. His wife comes in with another plant.

LAWRENCE: Who was that at the door?

FRIEDA: A woman from the village who wanted to see you. I sent her away.

LAWRENCE: Call her back.

FRIEDA: Don't waste your strength on strange women.

LAWRENCE: I don't intend to waste my strength on her. I just want to hear what nonsense she has to say. Catch her before she starts back down the hill, and take that plant out with you. There's too many plants already—they eat up the air.

FRIEDA: *Ahh, mein Gott—sehr gut!*

[She goes back out with the plant. Lawrence continues his needle-work. After a few moments a spinsterish looking woman of thirty-five steals diffidently across the threshhold bearing a little potted geranium. She halts by the door and stares at Lawrence with fascination in terror. The small plant vibrates in her hand.]

LAWRENCE *[sharply]*: Don't bring that thing in here!

VISITOR [*gasping*]: Oh, I beg your—!

LAWRENCE: Set it out that door. [*He indicates the door on the terrace.*]

VISITOR: — Oh! [*The visitor scurries to the door and bends awkwardly to set the plant outside.*]

LAWRENCE [*glancing distastefully at her*]: Goodness! You American women don't know how to move, you're not at home in your bodies.

VISITOR: I beg your pardon?

LAWRENCE: Sit down.

VISITOR [*nervously*]: Where shall I sit?

LAWRENCE: There's only one chair besides this one here which is occupied by myself.

[*She seizes the little wicker chair and bears it uncertainly toward Lawrence. She is undetermined at just what distance to place herself. Lawrence watches these diffident maneuvers with some amusement.*]

LAWRENCE: Mrs.—?

VISITOR: Miss!

LAWRENCE: Preston?

VISITOR: No, Peabody! Ariadne Peabody.

LAWRENCE: I must ask you to move that chair. You've just created a total eclipse of the sun.

VISITOR [*scrambling aside with the chair*]: Oh, I'm dreadfully sorry.

[*She is now almost behind him.*]

LAWRENCE [*dryly*]: This chair of mine is a very difficult chair to move about, and if we are going to carry on any kind of conversation, I'm afraid you will have to remain within range of my vision.

VISITOR [*scrambling back to original position*]: Oh, my goodness, *excuse* me!

LAWRENCE: Most of you American women speak so indistinctly one has to watch your lips to get the slightest idea of what you're gabbing about. [*Looks at her.*] I'm sorry but now you're back in the way of the sun.

VISITOR [*desperately*]: Oh, gracious!

LAWRENCE: Don't move again or you'll certainly make me dizzy. —Just take off that hat.

[*Visitor jerks off her hat.*]

LAWRENCE: Now you've gone and disarranged your hair.

VISITOR: Oh, goodness, have I really?

LAWRENCE: Have I any reason to misinform you about it? Come over here.

VISITOR: Pardon?

LAWRENCE: Please come over so I can fix it for you. I always fix my wife's when she gets it messed, for one thing I can't endure is an untidy woman.

[*She rises uncertainly.*]

LAWRENCE [*clapping his hands*]: *Vite, vite!* You can certainly see that I'm not in condition to rape you, even in case I had that inclination. Bend over—stoop! It only takes a second.

[*The visitor bends awkwardly. Lawrence jerks her hair roughly back from her forehead.*]

VISITOR [*gasping*]: Oh!

LAWRENCE: A little pulling is very good for the scalp—improves circulation. [*Adjusts the hairpins*] There now—very much better. Go back there and sit down.

[*The visitor, slightly dazed, returns to her chair.*]

LAWRENCE: I'll go on with my work. How do you like this pattern?

VISITOR: What is it?

LAWRENCE: The original male and female. —You see how depraved I am? I even put sex in my sewing.

[*Visitor laughs breathlessly and straightens her skirt.*]

LAWRENCE: Come on—Why don't you start talking?

VISITOR [*in a rush*]: Oh, Mr. Lawrence, I don't know where to begin.

LAWRENCE: You have a great deal to say?

VISITOR: Oh, so much, so much!

LAWRENCE: Well, you'd better get started, you can't stay all afternoon.

VISITOR: Ever since I first started to read your books—

LAWRENCE: You knew that here was a man you could bare your soul to?

VISITOR: Yes!

LAWRENCE: Well, bare it, bare it! I'm ready to give it a detailed examination.

VISITOR: I—I—!

LAWRENCE: Tell me about your lover.

VISITOR: I don't have any.

LAWRENCE: Nonsense. Everyone has, even if it's just an old felt bedroom slipper. How about that man you met on the boat six years ago last August?

VISITOR: Two years ago!

LAWRENCE: So recently?

VISITOR: How did you know?

LAWRENCE: His shadow is plainly visible in your eyes. What was his name?

VISITOR: If only I knew! That would solve the whole problem.

LAWRENCE: Tch, tch. You should always ask. Was it completed?

VISITOR: What?

LAWRENCE: The act.

VISITOR: What act, Mr. Lawrence?

LAWRENCE [*with a satyrical grin*]: Ahh—Miss Innocence!

VISITOR: It wasn't an act, Mr. Lawrence, but only a meeting.

LAWRENCE: Hmmm. The pernicious effect of sterile intellectualism again. Back when the world was young and man was a red-blooded animal every meeting resulted in an act of one kind or another. Now meetings are simply meetings, stiff little bows and hypocritical smiles and a little small talk on the weather. All the natural healthy venom we have in our natures, instead of having immediate, spontaneous expression in little fights between neighbors, is all stored up in a sort of national reserve till it becomes convenient for the heads of states to release it in the grand-scale lunacy of war. All because it is no longer considered proper to slap a man in the face because you don't like the cut of his features or throw a girl in the ditch because you *do* like *hers*. But that's a little bit off the subject, ain't it? This man you met on the steamship from Hong Kong to Sydney, Australia?

VISITOR: Oh, no, indeed, no! It was just on the ferry from Oakland to San Francisco.

LAWRENCE: Oh. And I suppose the last night out you dined together at the Captain's table?

VISITOR: I'm afraid you don't understand.

LAWRENCE: Now you're being offensive. I understand all that there is to be understood. He occupied the seat adjoining yours?

VISITOR: Oh, no, we stood together at the rail—

LAWRENCE: Vomiting?

VISITOR: Gracious, no!

LAWRENCE: The idea amused me a little. And this young man, was he handsome?

VISITOR: I haven't the least idea, but that doesn't matter.

LAWRENCE: You didn't look at him?

VISITOR: Not exactly. I was too dazed to look.

LAWRENCE: You were breathless and blind and very nearly unconscious.

VISITOR: You are not—making fun of me—Mr. Lawrence?

LAWRENCE: No.

VISITOR: Please don't. It's a serious matter.

LAWRENCE: Quite. He was small and shy?

VISITOR: Ho, he was large and very, very *forward*.

LAWRENCE: He nudged you slightly?

VISITOR: Not slightly at all, Mr. Lawrence. —He openly embraced me.

[*Pause.*]

LAWRENCE: *Ugh!*

VISITOR: What's that, Mr. Lawrence?

LAWRENCE: Ugh?—That's just a little idiomatic expression that I picked up among the Indians, Miss Preston. It indicates all kinds of emphatic reactions. And this embrace that you mention—I wonder if you could describe it?

VISITOR: His arm went around my waist—

LAWRENCE: Yes?

VISITOR: His fingers pressed me!

LAWRENCE: Where?

VISITOR [*delicately touching her right side*]: Here.

LAWRENCE: Not *too* forward, was he?

VISITOR: Forward enough, I should say.

LAWRENCE: And you, I suppose—I suppose you responded with a delicate pressure of his arm. —Or maybe rotated the tip of your index finger in the cup of his palm?

VISITOR: Indeed I did not, Mr. Lawrence. I made no response whatsoever!

LAWRENCE: Because of modesty?

VISITOR: No—Paralysis!

LAWRENCE: Oh. —One of those rare electrical things between people. He made no remarks?

VISITOR: What?

LAWRENCE: The man said nothing, nothing occurred except the tentative pressure?

VISITOR: It very shortly ceased to be tentative even.

LAWRENCE: The pressure, you mean?

VISITOR: Yes!

LAWRENCE: Was removed?

VISITOR: No—on the contrary.

LAWRENCE: Became quite definite?

VISITOR: *Yes!* [*She leans forward.*]

LAWRENCE: And still he said nothing?

VISITOR: Nothing!

LAWRENCE: And you said nothing?

VISITOR: I cleared my throat three times but I couldn't speak.

LAWRENCE: Never a single word was uttered between you?

VISITOR: Not till the ferryboat landed at San Francisco.

LAWRENCE: Then he—

VISITOR: Then he—released me. And then he—finally—*spoke!*

LAWRENCE: Distinctly?

VISITOR: In a whisper.

LAWRENCE: Whispered *what?*

VISITOR: He whispered his name which I can't remember and—Seven o'clock!

LAWRENCE: Seven o'clock?

VISITOR: Yes!

LAWRENCE: Presumably the hour of the inherited assignation?

VISITOR: Presumably.

LAWRENCE: And that was all he whispered, only his name and the time?

VISITOR: The time and also the place.

LAWRENCE: He also mentioned the place?

VISITOR: He also mentioned the name of a certain hotel.

LAWRENCE: And you did what?

VISITOR: I nodded.

LAWRENCE: Affirmatively?

VISITOR: Yes!

LAWRENCE: You kept the appointment?

VISITOR [*jumping up*]: No, no, no, I couldn't!

LAWRENCE [*wheeling his chair angrily toward her*]: Scruples? Belated scruples?

VISITOR [*retreating*]: No, no, not that!

LAWRENCE: What then? Interference by relatives?

VISITOR: No, no, no! No relatives!

LAWRENCE: Illness? Accident?

VISITOR: No!

LAWRENCE: Paralysis?

VISITOR: *No!* You'll laugh when I tell you—

LAWRENCE: What?

VISITOR: That I couldn't remember the name which he had whispered. That as soon as he disappeared I forgot his name. —I couldn't even remember the name of the place that he had told me to meet him! My brain was a blank, a blank! All that I knew was that somewhere in the city at half past five the man whom I had been waiting all of my life to meet—was waiting for *me*!

LAWRENCE: And just through a treacherous little defect of recollection—

VISITOR: I couldn't go to him—

LAWRENCE: —and realize the purpose of your existence!

[*Pause.*]

LAWRENCE: Dreadful . . . .

[*Visitor covers her face.*]

LAWRENCE: Pull yourself together, Miss—

VISITOR: —Peabody.

LAWRENCE: And tell me what happened after this incident on the ferry from—

VISITOR: Oakland.

LAWRENCE: To—?

VISITOR: San Francisco. It seemed to be hopeless and so I tried to forget. Not merely his name and the place but the whole affair. At first I thought that I *had* forgotten about it. Only I couldn't— concentrate anymore.

LAWRENCE: Not on anything?

VISITOR: No.

LAWRENCE: You had a position?

VISITOR: In a public library!

LAWRENCE: Lost it?

VISITOR: Yes. Children would ask for *The Rover Boys on the River* and I would give them *Women in Love* by you.

LAWRENCE: A subconscious effort to pull down public morals. Your health was shattered?

VISITOR: Completely.

LAWRENCE: Luckily you had been left some money in trust by an Aunt?

VISITOR: Not an Aunt—an Uncle.

LAWRENCE: So you could travel?

VISITOR: Yes.

LAWRENCE: And you traveled and traveled and still the pains persisted?

VISITOR: How did you know of the pains?

LAWRENCE: Of course there were pains! Where were the pains located?

VISITOR: Here in my side.

LAWRENCE: There in the side where he touched you!

VISITOR: Yes, in the side where he touched me!

LAWRENCE: You thought at first—?

VISITOR: That it was appendicitis!

LAWRENCE: You had it removed?

VISITOR: Yes, they removed my appendix.

LAWRENCE: And found it healthy?

VISITOR: Found it perfectly healthy.

LAWRENCE: After that—?

VISITOR: Of course the pains persisted.

LAWRENCE: Of course the pains still persisted. And then—?

[*Visitor covers her face.*]

LAWRENCE: You begin to doubt that it was a physical thing.

[*Visitor nods.*]

LAWRENCE: You came to realize what was the matter with you? Your modesty and your pride were no longer quite strong enough to conceal the true facts from you? The censor broke down and the blinding truth came through! These pains had started the night that the stranger pressed you! They were a souvenir of a ride on a ferry-boat, weren't they?

VISITOR: Yes! Yes—yes, they were!

LAWRENCE [*triumphantly*]: Ahhh.

VISITOR: But that's an old story now. That came out the first time I was put under.

LAWRENCE: Hypnosis, you mean?

VISITOR: Yes, hypnosis.

LAWRENCE: And still the pains persisted.

VISITOR: At intervals—yes. Whenever I got near the water.

LAWRENCE: Why don't you avoid the water?

VISITOR: It has a—

LAWRENCE: Fatal attraction?

VISITOR: Not exactly fatal but—

LAWRENCE: Definitely an attraction?

VISITOR: Yes—an attraction.

LAWRENCE: So why did you come to me?

VISITOR: Because of your books. You've written so much about—sex.

LAWRENCE: I never wrote about sex. What I write about is the phallic reality. Sex is cerebral, intellectual, sex is in the head. The phallic reality is located in the—

VISITOR: Yes?

LAWRENCE: I don't wish to give you an ear-ache, Miss Preston. [*Seriously.*] You are the victim of hundreds of years of wrong-thinking. Prudery, shame, sterile intellectualism denying the body, pointing shame at the flesh! Let me tell you before I send you away— My great religion is a belief in the blood, the body's superior wisdom to that of the mind. We can go wrong in our minds.

But what our blood feels and believes and says is always true. That is all, Miss Preston. —You may go now.

VISITOR: But, Mr. Lawrence, I hoped that you would help— I hoped that you could tell me what to do.

LAWRENCE: Your only course of action, Miss Preston, is plainly apparent. You've simply got to find the man on the ferry.

VISITOR: How can I when I don't remember his name?

LAWRENCE: But you *do* remember his name. What *was* his name, Miss Preston?

[*Pause*]

VISITOR [*in a sudden whisper*]: O'Reilly! [*Breathlessly repeating.*] —O'Reilly, O'Reilly, Adam O'Reilly! [*Shouting jubilantly.*] Oh, Mr. Lawrence, now, now, now I remember! His name was Adam O'Reilly!

LAWRENCE: The hotel? Quick, quick! —The hotel!

VISITOR: O'Reilly—the Golden Gate Hotel—room ten hundred and twenty! [*She begins to run wildly about the room.*] My hat! My gloves! My beaded bag! Where are they?

LAWRENCE: Here! [*He tosses her the huge straw hat.*] Now where are you going?

VISITOR: I'm going back—back to Adam! San Francisco! — The Golden Gate Hotel! Room ten hundred and twenty! *Ohhhhhh*—! Goodbye, Mr. Lawrence! [*She flies out the door to the terrace.*]

[*Lawrence chuckles and picks up his needlework. Frieda comes in and steals up softly behind him and rests her chin on his head.*]

FRIEDA [*tenderly*]: What are you working on, darling?

LAWRENCE: Adam and Eve—on a San Francisco ferry. . . .

CURTAIN

AND TELL SAD STORIES OF THE DEATHS OF QUEENS...

(A PLAY IN TWO SCENES)

And Tell Sad Stories of the Deaths of Queens... was first performed by the Shakespeare Theatre on April 22, 2004, at the Kennedy Center in Washington D.C. It was directed by Michael Kahn; the set design was by Andrew Jackness; the costume design was by Catherine Zuber; the lighting design was by Howell Binkley; the sound design was by Martin Desjardins; and original music was composed by Adam Wernick. The cast, in order of appearance, was as follows:

CANDY DELANEY	Cameron Folmar
KARL	Myk Watford
ALVIN KRENNING	Hunter Gilmore
JERRY JOHNSON	Brian McMonagle

SCENE ONE

Scene: The beginning of Mardi Gras weekend in the French Quarter of New Orleans. The curtain rises on a living-room lighted by the soft blue dusk of a Southern spring, coming through French doors open upon a patio which is a tiny replica of a Japanese garden: fish-pool, fountain, weeping willow and even a short arched bridge with paper lanterns. The interior is also Japanese, or pseudo-Japanese, with bamboo furniture, very low tables, grass-mats, polished white or pale blue porcelain bowls and vases containing artificial dogwood or cherry blossoms and log silver stems of pussy-willow, everything very delicate and pastel. A curtain of beads or bamboo separates a small bedroom, upstage. A mechanical piano plays "Poor Butterfly," off-key, till the entrance of Candy, a New Orleans "queen" uncomfortably close to his thirty-fifth birthday with the sort of face that can never look adult, a grace and slimness that will always suggest a girlish young boy. The effeminacy of Candy is too natural, too innate, to require expression in mannerisms or voice: the part should be played without caricature.

Before Candy enters, as the piano expires, we hear a key's nervous scratch: then Candy's breathless voice—

CANDY [*offstage*]: I can never work a door key! No matter how long I occupy an apartment I still have trouble with door keys.

[*The door opens. Candy enters followed by a big, young merchant seaman, Karl.*]

CANDY: Come in, come on in!

KARL [*with suspicion*]: What's this?

CANDY: My apartment.

KARL: It looks like a chop suey joint.

CANDY: I did it all over this Spring in a sort of Japanese style. I want you to take a look at the patio first so I can close the doors and discourage a call from my tenants. I have tenants upstairs, a very nice pair of boys from Alabama. But whenever I entertain they have a way of dropping down uninvited, if you know what I mean. They make themselves a little too much at home here.

KARL: You own this place?

CANDY [*fast, excited*]: Yes, I own three pieces of property in the Quarter, this one and two others, all in good locations, rental property. The one on Chartres has six rental units including the slave-quarters and the one on Dumaine, four units: entire slave-quarters occupied by one tenant: a real show-place, I'll show it to you right after Mass tomorrow. Mr. Frazier, the tenant's in Biloxi, spends every week-end there. [*Winks.*] Has a friend at the air-base. And then, of course, I have my shop on Saint Charles just a block from Lee Circle, on this side of Lee Circle, a half hour's walk each way but very good for my figure. [*Laughs.*] Take a look at my lovely patio, Karl.

KARL: I can see it from here.

CANDY: Well, we'll slip out later: the air's such a lovely soft blue, like a—Luna moth's wing. Just step outside for one moment.

[*Karl ambles out.*]

CANDY: Don't talk out loud, just whisper—or my tenants will come flying downstairs, especially if they see you . . .

KARL: You mentioned a shop? You said you got a shop?

CANDY: Oh, yes.

KARL: What shop?

CANDY: Interior decorating. I told you. You don't remember?

KARL: No. I forgot.

CANDY: I had a business partner till just lately, a very nice older man who used to be my sponsor. We had a beautiful relationship for seventeen years. He brought me out in Atlanta, that long ago. I've had a very protected life till lately. [*Darts back in.*] Here he is, this is him. [*Snatches up a framed photo.*] Left his wife for me, sold out his business in Atlanta and we moved here in the war-years when I was eighteen, and he set me up in this shop and made me his partner in it. Well, nothing lasts forever. You dream that it will but it don't—I'll shut these doors so my tenants don't come flying down, now . . . [*He shuts the patio doors.*] No, nothing goes on forever. I worshipped Sidney Korngold. I never even noticed that he got heavy . . . . But Sidney had the aging man's weakness for youth . . . . I understood. I didn't even resent it—oh, I had a nervous collapse when he left but I didn't reproach him for it, I put no financial obstacles in his way, I made no demands, I said, I said to him: "Sid? Whatever makes you happy is what I want for you, daddy . . . " [*He sets the framed photo down with a lost look.*] —If my tenants come down to the door, don't make a sound till they go.

KARL: Girls?

CANDY: Women? Oh, no, I'd never rent to women again in my life, they're not only very slow payers, they're messy and destructive. No. These tenants are a pair of boys from Alabama: young queens, of course. I'd never consider renting to anyone else. Queens make wonderful tenants, take excellent care of the place, sometimes improve it for you. They are great home-lovers and have creative ideas. They set the styles and create the taste for the country. Don't you know that?

KARL: No.

CANDY: Just imagine this country without queens in it. It would be absolutely barbaric. Look at the homes of normal married couples. No originality: modern mixed with period, everything bunched around a big TV set in the parlor. Mediocrity is the passion among them. Conformity. Convention. Now I know the faults of queens, nobody knows the faults of queens better than I do.

KARL: Queens?

CANDY: What?

KARL: Are you queer?

CANDY: —*Baby,* are you *kidding?!!*

KARL: How about answering the question?

CANDY: Oh, now, really!

KARL: Huh?

CANDY: I thought that was understood in the first five minutes' talk we had in the bar.

KARL: You think I would be here if I'd thought you was a queer?

CANDY: Karl, I like you. I like you and I admire you. But really . . .

KARL: Really what?

CANDY: You can't expect me to seriously believe that a man who has been shipping in and out of New Orleans for five years is still not able to recognize a queen in a gay bar.

KARL: I don't go with queers.

CANDY: I know you don't. I'll tell you something. This is not the first time I have seen you. I mean this night. I have been noticing you off and on, here and there, ever since you started shipping out of this city. But up till lately I led a different life. I told you about my husband. When he broke with the normal world and took up with me as my sponsor, eighteen years ago, he changed his name. You wouldn't think it possible for any man to undergo such a complete transformation, new name, new life, new tastes and habits, even a new appearance. [*Turns his attention to the photo again.*] I mean he—ha ha!—not an old picture, either. Taken two years ago, slightly less. When he turned fifty. Remarkable? Would you guess it? Doesn't he look a fast thirty? I gave that man a new lease on life. I swear that when he started going with me in Atlanta, Georgia, he was a nondescript person, already a middle-aged one! Well . . . I never cheated on him. I'm the monogamous type. He did the cheating. And I was so trustful I didn't suspect it till after it had been going on for years . . . — Well, change is the heart of existence. I hold no grudge against him. We broke things off in a very dignified way. We had a joint bank account. I bought out his share of the business with my half of the money and he is now in Houston with his new chick, starting all over again, and I wish him luck with it. However he's picked a wrong one. But infatuation is even blinder than love. Specially when the victim is at the dangerous age like he is . . . [*Returns photograph to the bureau.*] —Well, he'll wake up soon and realize that he let a good thing go for one that's basically rotten. Just younger . . . Are you lookin' fo' somethin'?

KARL: Ain't you got something to drink?

CANDY: I've got just about the best-stocked liquor cabinet in the French Quarter, baby.

KARL: Now you're talkin'.

CANDY: I don't entertain very often but when I do, it's done well. You can depend on that. Let's see, you were drinkin' blended whiskey.

KARL: Never mind what I was drinkin'. I can switch without effort.

CANDY: Want something exotic?

KARL: Such as what, huh?

CANDY: Well, now, I could make you a Pimm's Cup number one, with a dash of Pernod, and cucumber slices and all. I could make you a golden dawn which is a pineapple rum drink. I could make you a—

KARL: How 'bout just pouring me a healthy shot of old Grandad.

CANDY: Now you're talkin', that's the way to talk. In a little while now, when I hear my tenants go out for their nightly cruise, we'll adjourn to the patio. It will be magical then, blue dusk. I have a Hi-Fi with a speaker in the garden and in the middle of my fishpool is an island with a willow that makes a complete curtain, an absolutely private retreat from the world except for a few little glimpses of sky now and then . . .

KARL: You sure do go in for fancy talk, Bud.

CANDY [*laughing*]: Yes, I do, but y'know it's natural to me. I ornament the language so to speak. I used to write poetry once. Still do sometimes when I'm feeling sentimental.

KARL: Ain't you drinkin'?

CANDY: No. I never drink.

KARL: Why's that?

CANDY: Would you guess I have a weight problem?

KARL: You look thin to me.

CANDY: Thank you. I am.

KARL: Then why have you got a weight problem?

CANDY: Because I must starve myself to keep my figure. No calorie goes uncounted.

KARL: Jesus! —You're a card.

CANDY: The joker in the deck?

KARL: —Naw. —The queen . . .

CANDY: I like you very much. I feel safe with you.

KARL: That's a mistake. Nobody's safe around me when I'm liquored up.

CANDY: I think I would be. I think you like me, too.

KARL: You're going to be disappointed.

CANDY: I don't think so.

KARL: You're not going to get what you're after.

CANDY: How do you know what I'm after?

KARL: You're different, but not that different. You want to be laid, and you won't be, not by me.

CANDY: You see? You've misunderstood me, it's happened already, just as it always does. I'd love to have anything at all between us but I would be just as happy with your true friendship, true and lasting, as with a mutual thing between us in bed. That's true. I would. I swear it.

KARL: Then you're different all right.

[*During this or his next long speech, Candy goes through the bamboo curtain into the bed area.*]

CANDY: Yes, I told you I was. I'm going to tell you something which you may think is a lie. You are only the second man in my life. The first was Mr. Sidney Korngold. He brought me out in Atlanta. When I was a chicken. Just as dumb as they come, knew there was something wrong with me but not I was queer. This man stopped me on Peachtree Street in Atlanta and asked me if I was a girl or a boy. He thought that I was a girl in boy's clothes. I told him that I was a boy, indignantly. He said, "Come home with me." However he didn't take me to his home. Mr. Korngold was a respectable married man with two kiddies. However he had this double life downtown. He took me to a suite in a hotel. Which he kept under a different name. Opened a closet containing girl's clothes and wigs. Told me to get into something. I did, including the wig. And he seduced me . . .

KARL: Yeah?

CANDY: What he didn't know: his wife had put a tail on him, a private dick. She sued him for a divorce, naming me as the correspondent. It was not a public trial, to keep it private he had to sell his business and give this woman everything that he owned. We left Atlanta together. He was my sponsor. He put me up in business, I already had a talent for decorating. I felt obliged to make good, and I did, I made good. This was eighteen years ago. We remained together for seventeen years. Only last year we broke up. I discovered that he'd been cheating on me in spite of the fact that I'd been completely faithful. It broke my heart. I have pride. I bought out his share in the business with my half of our joint bank account and started from scratch on my own. He went to Texas with his new chick. People follow set patterns. Over and over. Haven't you noticed they do?

KARL: —What're you doing in there?

CANDY: Changing clothes. And sex. [*He emerges in drag.*] I am a transvestite. Here I am.

KARL: —Are you crazy?

CANDY: No. Just very abnormal I guess.

KARL: Well, I got to admit—

CANDY: —What?

KARL: You're as much like a woman as any real one I seen.

CANDY: Thank you. That's the object.

KARL: Sure you're not one?

CANDY: Want me to show you?

KARL: No.

CANDY: How is your drink, does it need freshening, yet?

KARL: Yeah. I'm a very heavy drinker.

CANDY: You'll notice I'm being very feminine now in my talk and my mannerisms as well as appearance. Isn't that what you want?

KARL: You do this often?

CANDY: Often when I'm alone. In fact usually when I'm alone, when I come in at night, I put on my hair and slip in a fresh negligée. I have ten of them in all the rainbow colors, some of them worth a small fortune. Ha ha, not a small fortune, I mean a hundred or two . . .

KARL: You must be loaded.

CANDY: Rich? No, just well off. My life expectancy isn't a long one and I see no reason to put aside much for the so-called rainy day.

KARL: You're sick?

CANDY: Haven't you noticed how short-winded I am? I have a congenital heart. I mean a congenital defect of the heart. A leakage that gradually leaks more. It's just as well. I won't look pretty much longer, even in 'drag' . . . . One of my upstairs tenants, the younger one, is a poet. Let me read you a poem he wrote about queers which I think is lovely, not great, no, but lovely. [*Produces and reads lyric.*]

I think the strange, the crazed, the queer
will have their holiday this year,
I think, for just a little while,
There will be pity for the wild.

I think in places known as gay,
In special little clubs and bars,
Pierrot will serenade pierrot
with frantic drums and sad guitars.

I think for some uncertain reason
mercy will be shown this season
To the lovely and misfit,
To the brilliant and deformed.

I think they will be housed and warmed
and fed and comforted a while,
Before, with such a tender smile,
The earth destroys her crooked child.

—That's it. It's dedicated to me, just to my initials, it's going to come out in a little mag soon. He's the nicer of my upstairs tenants. They occupy the slave quarters. When they go out I will show you their place because it's one of my best interiors, and very ingenious in the use of small space, only two rooms and a— You look unhappy! Why?

KARL: Do you know any women?

CANDY: Won't I do?

KARL: No, I don't go this route.

CANDY: I told you, I just want friendship. I'm terribly lonely. Just to have the company of someone I find so attractive, to entertain him, amuse him, is all that I ask for! Really!

KARL: You're a new one, but the pitch is familiar.

CANDY: I don't deny for a moment that if you suddenly sprang up and seized me in your arms! —I wouldn't resist . . .

KARL: You're barking up the wrong tree, in the wrong woods, in the wrong country.

CANDY: I only said if you did. I didn't imply it was probable that you would. I didn't even imply that it was—likely . . . You like some music?

KARL: Yeah, turn on some music.

CANDY: What's your preference in music, popular or classic or—what do you like?

KARL: —I don't care, anything . . .

CANDY [*reading an album title*]: *Waltzing with Wayne King.*

KARL: Good.

CANDY [*after the music begins*]: —I'm told I follow divinely. Shall we dance?

KARL: No.

CANDY: Why? Why not? Come on!

KARL: You look like a girl but I can't forget you're not one.

CANDY: You will when you start dancing with me. Are you afraid to?

KARL: Oh, well . . . [*Rises and dances with her.*]

CANDY: Oh, oh, oh . . .

KARL: You sure can follow okay.

CANDY: Doin' what comes naturally!

KARL [*quitting*]: I can't. I just can't. Ha ha! —It seems too—

CANDY: Too what, honey?

KARL: —unnatural—not right. —I'd better go.

CANDY: *OH, NO!—NO!!*

KARL: Yeah, I think so.

CANDY: Don't be so conventional and inhibited, why, what for!? You force me to bring up a matter which is always embarrassing. Are you hard up for money?

KARL: I got a few dollars on me.

CANDY: That's not enough for a Mardi Gras weekend, baby.

KARL: Oh, I'll make out. I'll probably meet some dame over forty or fifty at Pat's or somewhere. Maybe even a B-girl who'll take my tab, and—

CANDY: She wouldn't be pretty as I am.

KARL: She'd be female.

CANDY: But would she offer you all?

KARL: What's all?

CANDY: All that I've got to offer. This lovely place at your disposal now and always. Unlimited credit at every bar in the quarter. Cash, too. A pocketful of it. And more where that pocketful came from. And no strings, Karl. Your freedom.

KARL: I want a woman tonight, having been at sea for six weeks.

CANDY: I can fix that too.

KARL: How?

CANDY: Most of my close friends are women, and all are attractive.

KARL: You mean you can fix me up with a good looking girl?

CANDY: Easy as pie.

KARL: What would you get out of it? What would you want for all this?

CANDY: Just your companionship, later. When you come home.

KARL: My home in this town is a bed at the Salvation Army dormitory on Rampart.

CANDY: This is your home, if you'll take it.

KARL: I like to pay my own way unless I am giving something. I'm not giving nothing to you.

CANDY: You'd come home drunk. Fall in bed. I would take

your shoes off, just your shoes, and blissfully fall asleep with your hand in mine.

KARL: For Christ's sake.

CANDY: No, for mine!

KARL: You're crazy. I'm going now.

CANDY: You don't believe I could fix you up with a girl who would be everything that you dream of?

KARL: It's all part of a plot. I just want some money from you. You can have what you want, now, for ten dollars. Let's get it over with, huh?

CANDY: But what I told you I wanted is what I want.

KARL: It's all you'd get.

CANDY: I know it.

KARL: And it would cost you twenty.

CANDY: Twenty's nothing. Give me your empty wallet.

[*He does. She removes bills from a teapot and puts them in his wallet. She puts the wallet in his pocket. He takes it out and carefully counts the bills. She has given him fifty dollars. He grunts. She has picked up the phone and dialed a number. She gets a response.*]

CANDY [*into the receiver*]: I want to speak to Helene.

KARL: Who's Helene?

CANDY: Stripper at the Dragon.

KARL: You mean really one of those strip-teasing dolls?

CANDY: Wait and see, I deliver! Helene? Candy! How are you? How about coming over between shows, honey? There's someone here you'll adore. Six foot two, eyes of blue, magnificent, young, and loaded! — Sure. — How much? — It's a deal.

KARL: How much!

CANDY [*covering phone*]: On me! [*Uncovers phone.*] How soon? [*Turns to Karl.*] Nine-thirty. Okay?

KARL: That's three hours from now.

CANDY: You need to shave and shower and catch forty winks, while I prepare a shrimp curry such as you've never tasted. What have you got to lose?

KARL: All right. But just don't—

CANDY [*into phone*]: Fine, honey. I'll expect you. [*She hangs up, walks to the shutter doors, and throws them open on the transparent blue dusk of the Japanese patio-garden.*] Now is the hour, just now, to go in my garden!

KARL: This is the queerest deal I ever got into. What I want is another shot of that bourbon.

CANDY: Go in the garden. Cross the fishpool on the Japanese bridge. Sit down on the little Eighteenth century bench beneath the willow. Spring has come, this is the first evening of it! I'm going to put on my chiffon! Before you've counted to fifty, I'll bring you a drink.

KARL: Remember that you'll get nothing.

CANDY: Getting nothing is something I never forget.

[*Karl nods and goes out.*]

KARL: —Is this thing safe to walk on?

CANDY: Strong as steel! Guaranteed!

KARL: —Well, if it breaks, it won't be the only thing that breaks around here.

CANDY: Ha ha ha!

KARL [*on the bridge*]: It's creaking. [*He completes crossing.*] Well, I made it. Hurry up with the drink.

CANDY: Start counting. [*She has started changing into a long, pale yellow chiffon.*] Before you get to fifty I'll—

[*Knock at door.*]

CANDY: —Who's there?

ALVIN'S VOICE AT THE DOOR: Krenning.

CANDY: Go away, Krenning. [*Catches her breath.*] I'm not alone tonight!

ALVIN [*outside the door*]: Are you safe?

CANDY: Perfectly.

ALVIN: Sure?

CANDY: Certain!

ALVIN: Jerry saw him come in. He says he's dirt.

CANDY: Tell that jealous bitch to mind her own little business for a change!

ALVIN: He says he's the one that broke Tiny Henderson's jaw which is still wired together.

CANDY: Tell her I appreciate her concern but I am not Henderson and I am not with dirt. You all cruise every night and bring home trick after trick which I put up with despite the chance I'm taking of a terrible scandal. This is the first person I've brought into my house since I broke up with my husband! Go away! Go away! —I'm with someone I love!

ALVIN: —Good luck.

CANDY: —Go away! [*She pours bourbon and goes out to the garden.*]

[*The lights dim. A splash is heard, followed by continual cursing and a continual murmur of solicitude. As the lights come back up, Karl comes back inside, dripping wet. There are loud, enquiring cries from a gallery above.*]

CANDY [*outside, calling back*]: Will you all mind your own business fo' a change?

[*Candy goes back inside, shutting and locking the French doors. Then she rushes up to Karl. The enquiring cries have turned to shrill giggles and cackles.*]

CANDY: Bitches! Didn't I tell you?

KARL: You goddam faggots.

CANDY: Oh, now—

KARL: Oh, now what? This is going to cost you, Sister.

CANDY: Don't be mad at Candy! How did I know it wasn't built for a man? You take those wet things off and slip into the loveliest Chinese robe you've ever laid your blue eyes on!

KARL: Chinese shit.

CANDY: Isn't it lucky you had on dungarees?

KARL: You ain't gonna think it's so lucky before I go. I want you to know I'm takin' over this place.

CANDY: —That's just what I want you t'do.

KARL: I bet you'd dance with pleasure if I knocked you around. I'd gladly do it, too. Except you'd enjoy it too much. Where is this robe?

[*They have retired behind the bamboo curtain and the wet dungarees, wadded, are hurled through it.*]

KARL: And you stay away, *way* away! —Blondie.

CANDY: My name is not Blondie, it's Candy.

KARL: —Some candy . . .

CANDY: Now you just dry you'self off, since you're so touchy, and slip into this heavenly Chinese robe, while I mix you a violet. Know what a violet is? It's Pernod and vodka, mixed, on the rocks! —The strongest drink ever made. —That's why it's called a violet, I reckon . . .

KARL: I never been given a knock out that knocked me out before I knocked out the bitch that give it to me. —Keep that in mind! Don't forget it . . .

CANDY: Ha ha ha . . .

KARL: —Shit . . .

CANDY: I recognized your type the instant I met you. Big rough talking two hundred pounds of lonely, lost little boy.

KARL: —I recognized your type *before* I met you.

CANDY: I have no secrets! Do I?

KARL: I don't care what you have besides crabs and cash.

[*He comes out in a magnificent Chinese robe. Candy is mixing violets at a bamboo bar in a corner.*]

KARL: You got a phone here, ain't you?

CANDY: Right on the table beside you.

KARL [*finding it*]: Aw. [*Lifts ivory white French phone and dials a number.*]

CANDY: Who you callin', baby?

KARL: Where's my drink?

CANDY: Here, Sugar.

KARL [*into phone, taking drink*]: I wanna speak to a lady whose first name is Alice. I can't remember the last name, a redheaded lady that drives a white '52 Cadillac with North Carolina plates on it.

CANDY: Oh, I know who *that* is. Alice "Blue" Jackson, we call her.

KARL [*into phone*]: Oh. Her last name is Jackson. Yeah, Jackson . . . [*Then to Candy.*] Be careful what you say of her in front of me. Huh?

CANDY: I don't attack people's character when they're not present.

KARL: There's no woman as low as a faggot.

CANDY: You must've had some bad experiences with them.

KARL: I've had bad experiences with them and they've had worse experiences with me.

CANDY: You know, I think your bark is worse than your bite.

KARL: That's because—*Huh?*— [*Speaking into phone.*] Aw . . . Well, tell her to call this number. [*To Candy.*] What's your number?

CANDY: Magnolia 0347.

KARL: Magnolia 0347. —Soon's she comes in . . . [*He hangs up and drains glass.*]

CANDY: A violet ought to be sipped. [*Pause.*] You're going to like me. I know that you're going to like me. You already do. I can tell by your eyes when you look at me.

KARL: When I look at you I'm measuring you for a coffin.

CANDY: You're going to discover that Candy's your—

KARL: When did she say she'd get here?

CANDY: Nine-thirty.

KARL: What time's it now?

CANDY: Seven-fifteen.

KARL: Call me at nine. [*He goes to sleep in the next room.*]

One week later: a rainy winter Sunday morning in New Orleans. Candy, in drag, is having coffee and Knox gelatin in fruit juice at a daintily set breakfast table on which there is a pale blue Japanese vase of pussy willows. In the next room Karl is sleeping loudly. All of Candy's motions and actions are muted so as not to disturb the loud sleeper. Presently another queen, Jerry, enters without knocking. This one is still under thirty, is handsome but with a pinched look and a humorous lisp.

JERRY: Good morning and happy birthday to you, Miss Delaney.

CANDY: Quiet, please. [*She indicates bedroom with sleeper.*] Didn't I tell you he'd come back before Sunday.

[*Jerry starts towards bedroom.*]

CANDY: Stay out of the bedroom.

JERRY: I'm just taking a peek. [*He thrusts his head through the curtains and whistles softly.*]

CANDY: Come back out of the bedroom.

JERRY: I'm not in the bedroom.

CANDY: Everything in my life has been messed up by bitches, and I am sick of it.

JERRY: I was going to give you a birthday present.

CANDY: Please don't bother. Just don't mess up the only important thing in my life right now.

JERRY: I hope it lasts, Mother.

CANDY: And don't use bitch-talk in here. It's not only common, it's also very old-fashioned, it places and dates you. My name is Candy Delaney.

JERRY: Miss Delaney to me.

CANDY: Then get out of here, will you? —No. Wait. —Sit down. I want to talk to you seriously a minute. Things have got to change here because I will not have my happiness jeopardized by two bitches under my roof that think to be homosexual means to be cheap and common. And do the bars every night, and only think of new tricks.

JERRY: That's fine coming from you, the mother of us all, on her thirty-fifth birthday.

CANDY: Yes, I'm not young anymore. The queen-world is full of excitement for young queens only. For me its *passé,* and *finit.* I want to have some dignity in my life, and now I have found a person that I can live with on a *dignified* basis and on a *permanent* basis, who won't compromise me in my professional life, my career, and that I can give something to and who can give something to me, so that between us we can create a satisfactory new existence for both.

JERRY: You've got the birthday blues.

CANDY: I've never been so happy in my life.

JERRY: You've had a sad life, Mother.

CANDY: Will you please leave here and go to your own apartment and when your month is up I will appreciate it if you and that faggot you live with will please move out. Why don't you rent an apartment in the project?

JERRY: And I spent twenty bucks on your birthday present, Candy.

CANDY: Since I won't receive it it's safe for you to exaggerate what it cost you.

JERRY: —This is the last time you will ever insult me.

CANDY: I hope so.

[*Jerry exits, slamming the door. Karl wakes with a groan and comes stumbling into the kitchen.*]

CANDY: Baby, what d'ya want for breakfast?

KARL: You can mix me a violet.

CANDY: Baby, not for breakfast.

KARL: I know what I want for breakfast, don't try and tell me. Where's the Pernod bottle?

[*Candy rises with a sigh and produces the Pernod.*]

KARL: Where's the vodka?

[*Candy brings him the vodka.*]

KARL: Get me some ice-cubes in a big glass.

[*Candy brings him a glass with ice.*]

KARL: All right now. Drink your goddam coffee and leave me alone.

CANDY [*almost tearful*]: I hate to see you just flying into ruin, baby. You are too wonderful a person, and I love you.

KARL: When I'm at sea I go weeks without liquor.

CANDY: You are a wonderful, wonderful, beautiful person and you know I adore you?!

KARL: You're a slob.

CANDY: I don't think you mean that, baby.

KARL: Don't take any bets on it.

CANDY: Otherwise why would you be here?

[*Alvin Krenning silently opens the door and stands in it, ignored by the pair at the table.*]

KARL: I run out of money.

CANDY: That's just an excuse that you make for coming back to me last night.

KARL: If you think so, just try to get out of paying me for last night, and I mean plenty. Plenty!

ALVIN: Candy, I want to speak to you.

CANDY: I told your roommate not to come in this apartment without knocking at the door and that goes the same for you, Alvin.

ALVIN: You have hurt Jerry.

CANDY: I'm glad. If it made some impression.

ALVIN: What's gotten into you, Candy?

CANDY: I am fed up with bitches and bitch talk and bitch manners. Why do you think I did this apartment over?

[*Karl rises and starts toward a door.*]

CANDY: Where are you going, baby?

KARL: The head. [*He goes into the bathroom.*]

CANDY [*to Alvin*]: Sit down and have some coffee.

ALVIN: You have broke Jerry's heart.

CANDY: No, I haven't.

ALVIN: You have.

CANDY: I had to make it plain to him that from now on I want no tenants under my roof anymore that have no respect for what I am trying to do.

ALVIN: What are you trying to do? Ditch your old friends?

CANDY: There's nobody values old friends more than I do but I will not have them bitching my life up for me when I want to preserve the first true worthwhile relationship I have found since I broke up with Sidney.

ALVIN: If you're talking about Karl, just let me tell you something.

CANDY: You and Jerry cheat all the time on each other and can't stand to see me working out something decent.

[*Alvin rises with an angry shrug and starts out.*]

CANDY [*rising*] What were you going to tell me? I just want to know!

ALVIN [*turning at door*]: Karl was shacked up with a woman all last week while you were crying your heart out, and only returned to this place because she threw him out of her house on Saint Charles Street.

CANDY: A lie!

[*Alvin starts out.*]

CANDY: Who told you this story?

ALVIN: Nobody. I know it. I know the woman, and so do you. Alice Jackson.

CANDY: When Karl comes out of the bathroom I will ask him. Meanwhile I will appreciate it if you and Miss Johnson start packing. I will refund the rest of your rent for this month.

ALVIN: Jerry is packing already. [*He goes out, slamming the door.*]

CANDY [*rushing after him into hall, shouting*]: Remember I don't know you after this! Nowhere! On the street! [*She shuts the door. She is visibly shaken.*]

[*Karl comes out of bathroom with a towel, in damp shorts, and starts to dress.*]

KARL: What was that all about?

CANDY: I want to ask you a question. I've never lied to you, baby. I want you to tell me the truth. Have you had any connection with a woman this week?

KARL: Huh. What woman?

CANDY: A woman named Alice Jackson?

KARL: The answer is yes. What of it?

CANDY: Come over here and sit down at the table.

KARL: I'm dressing.

CANDY: You can dress later.

KARL: I can but I want to now. Okay?

CANDY: You are risking a wonderful future between us by not treating me with respect which I deserve from you. I have spent over three hundred dollars on you in the past week, at a time when I am just getting established in my own business, after long plans and great efforts! Let me tell you what I plan for us. First of all, I'm throwing out Alvin and Jerry and am redecorating this building to attract the highest class tenants. I own three pieces of property in the quarter and I have my own decorating place on Saint Charles Street. Is it or is it not true that you have been shacking up with this woman while you were not here last week, and lied about it, and told me you'd been to Biloxi with shipmates?

KARL: Can you think of any good reason for me to lie to you, fruitcake?

CANDY: Yes. I can, Butcher boy. You're not too drunk or hung over to know that I am the one, only me, that offers you a sound future. Just, just let me tell you the plans I've made for our future life together! I need a partner in business. You will be it. I'm going, in one year's time, to be the most high-paid, fashionable decorator in town. Wait! My talent is recognized! I did the TV show for the "Two Americas Fair."

[*Karl crosses to him and starts snapping his fingers.*]

CANDY [*ignoring Karl's gesture*]: Photographs of my interiors are going to be reproduced in *Southern Culture*'s next issue, *in color!—a full page spread!*

[*Karl continues snapping his fingers closer to Candy's face.*]

CANDY: Why are you snapping your fingers in my face?

KARL: The loot, give with the loot, I'm going.

CANDY: Where?

KARL: Alice's. We spent her month's allowance and that is why I come back here for one night only.

CANDY: You will stay *here* or get *nothing*!

KARL: You give the wrong answer, fruitcup.

[*Karl knocks her around, first lightly, then more severely. Candy's sobbing turns to stifled outcries.*]

KARL: Where do you keep it, where do you keep your loot, come on before I demolish you and the whole fucking pad!?

CANDY [*at last*]: Tea—pot, the—silver teapot . . .

[*Karl helps himself to a thick roll of greenbacks in the teapot and starts out.*]

KARL: Fill it back up. I might drop in here again the next time I ship in this town. [*He exits.*]

[*Candy has fallen to her knees but she crawls after him with surprising rapidity, shrieking his name over and over and louder and more piercingly each time. Jerry and Alvin burst in just as Candy topples lifelessly forward onto her face with a last strangulated outcry.*]

JERRY: Jesus, get her a drink. [*Alvin rushes to liquor cabinet as Jerry lifts Candy from floor.*] – Alvin? I think she's *dead*!

[*Alvin freezes with cognac bottle in hand.*]

JERRY: Help me get her on the goddam bed for Crissake.

ALVIN: Make it look like she died natural, Jerry.

JERRY: Will you shut up and take her legs, you cunt?

ALVIN [*obeying*]: We warned her, she wouldn't listen.

JERRY: She isn't breathing, she's gone.

ALVIN: We got to get her out of drag before the cops come, anyhow.

JERRY: Who's going to call the police? It's even too late for a priest.

ALVIN: Who do we notify? Korngold?

JERRY: Who is Korngold?

ALVIN: Her husband—separated—the one that left her— He went to Texas—Houston.

JERRY: Alvin? She's breathing: the brandy!

[*They pour brandy down her: she gags and retches. They laugh wildly.*]

ALVIN: Pull yourself together on your birthday!

CANDY [*sitting up slowly*]—Oh, my God. —I'm old! —I've gotten old, I'm old . . . .

[*Jerry motions Alvin to sit beside her. A pause: it begins to rain.*]

JERRY: Now let us sit upon a rumpled bed
           And tell sad stories of the deaths of queens . . .

[*Alvin and Jerry giggle. Finally even Candy joins in but her giggle turns to tears, as the scene dims out.*]

CURTAIN

NOTES ON THE TEXT

A NOTE ON WILLIAMS'S EARLIER ONE-ACT PLAYS

Sometime between January and July, 1941, Williams wrote optimistically about the short plays that he had been writing since the mid-to-late 1930s: "I may have some one-acts on Broadway – I hope they may prove to be the little glass slipper lost in my midnight scramble down the stairs."

Williams might well have considered success as a theme for fairy-tales in these dark months, the ones that followed the failed Boston production of his full-length play *Battle of Angels*. His hopeful allusion to himself as a potential Cinderella occurs in a fragmentary draft of unpublished correspondence, now filed in HRC (54.15), and addressed to Lawrence Langner of the Theatre Guild—which had mounted *Battle,* and which by July, 1941 had rejected its option to mount a revised version. However, the hopes that Williams cherished for his short plays in 1941 reflect his ongoing artistic priorities over a much longer period, from 1937 to 1943, when one-acts were an especially significant part of his dramatic production.

It is frequently observed that Williams used the short form as a laboratory for ideas to expand into longer plays. What is less often noticed is that he also conceived of his short scripts, especially during these years, as building blocks for the construction of cycles defined by shared thematic and regional elements. In most cases, Williams saw his early one-acts not just as individual experiments, but as possible components of full-length programs for submission to prospective producers and publishers. Among many projects of this kind that he formulated in his mind and in his notes, though without ever seeing them materialize on stage or in print, one was a large, evolving group of scripts he called *American Blues* (1937-1943 and later). Another was a smaller trilogy notionally entitled *Vieux Carré* (1941—not to be confused with the later, full-length play that Williams began in 1939 and completed in 1977).

Summer at the Lake, *The Big Game*, and *The Fat Man's Wife* are closely related by their common membership in a group of plays that Williams regarded collectively as a dramatic cycle, or group of scripts entitled *American Blues*. The idea germinated as early as April, 1937, when Williams wrote to Willard Holland concerning "some new one-acts" with this "compound title" (*Selected Letters* I, p. 94). In one of two drafts for a table of contents to *American Blues*, now filed at HRC (1.8), Williams named a number of works in progress as parts of this series. He clarified the concept by typing: "A program of one-act plays designed to approximate in dramaturgy the mood, atmosphere and meaning of American Blues music." This rationale for the title, *American Blues*, is a fascinating one and might well have been typed on a cover-sheet, now unlocated, to the set of four one-act plays that Williams submitted (along with three full-length plays) to a contest held by the Group Theatre in the winter of 1938-39.

On March 20, 1939, Molly Day Thacher wrote to award Williams a "special prize" of $100.00 for "the first three sketches" that he had entered in the Group Theatre competition under the title *American Blues*. In the letter, which is now filed at HRC (57.11, under Thacher's married name Kazan), Thacher also wrote: "Since there was no limitation as to the length of plays to be judged, we eliminated from consideration the fourth sketch in AMERICAN BLUES. It seems to us much inferior in quality to the first three, both in the writing and in the theatrical validity."

The version of *American Blues* entered in the Group Theatre contest certainly included *Moony's Kid Don't Cry*, and almost certainly included *The Dark Room*, according to evidence at HRC (61.8, letter from Roberta Barrett to William Kozlenko d. October 22, 1940) and in Williams's correspondence (*Selected Letters* I, p. 170). Furthermore, the tables of contents for *American Blues* now filed at HRC (1.8) feature the titles of *Hello From Bertha* and *The*

Long Goodbye in prominent positions, suggesting that these probably were the other two scripts that Williams submitted to the Group Theatre. If so, then all four of the original one-act submissions were to be published during the 1940s. However, the lists at HRC mention at least eight other titles as parts of *American Blues*. Among them are titles of at least three of the extant plays published here for the first time: *Summer at the Lake*, *The Fat Man's Wife*, and *The Big Game*. (One of the lists also includes the title "Escape," but this was probably meant to refer to *Summer at the Lake* by one of its original, alternate titles; see Note below.) It is possible, though unlikely that one or two of these, rather than *Hello From Bertha* and/or *The Long Goodbye*, were among the competition entries.

When in early 1939 the newly recognized Williams acquired his first real New York agent, Audrey Wood, she received the prize-winning *American Blues* plays from the Group Theatre and wrote to her brand-new client, lavishing welcome praise on what she called the "simple yet very true kind of character writing" in his one-acts. Wood told him, "Your attempt here to dramatize these different milieus comes off, in my opinion, very successfully" (*Leverich*, p. 303). Wood then began shopping around the four short scripts in the submitted version of *American Blues* to various venues, some of which proved unfruitful, such as Whit Burnett's *Story* magazine (*Selected Letters* I, p. 170).

Wood also tried to get Williams to send her still more of the short plays on which he had been working. The most likely reason for the existence of the tables of contents filed at HRC (1.8) is that those parts of *American Blues* which were bound together and circulating in 1939—i.e., those that Williams had entered in the competition—were prefaced with a list very much like them. Presumably, this is how Wood knew not only the texts of the plays that Williams had submitted to the Group Theatre, but also the titles of a number of other one-act plays in progress. Certainly she had asked about them soon after becoming his agent. In June, 1939, Williams responded to her inquiries: "The additional

'American Blues' sketches you mention are <u>existent</u> – that, however, is about the best that can be said for most of them, as they are mainly in the first draft and were not bound with the others because they did not seem ready for professional consideration. I am slowly adding, however, to these dramatic cross-sections and will send you new installments from time to time. The old ones listed on the frontispiece are all packed away among my <u>Mss</u>. in St. Louis and the next time I pass through there I'll see what I can excavate in the way of finished scripts" (*Selected Letters* I, p. 177).

In mid-1939 Williams left most of his recent drafts of one-acts at home with his parents while he was away in California. Those one-acts that had been included in the *American Blues* cycle, but not in the contest submission, lay fallow. Their author would not return to Missouri until September, 1939, and then only by way of heading toward New York City to meet Wood in person for the first time.

We do not know whether Williams ever supplied Wood with drafts of *The Big Game* or *The Fat Man's Wife*, but we may be sure that he sent the agency some version of *Summer at the Lake*, a play which he also continued revising in future years (see our Note to *Summer at the Lake*). In any event, it may be noted that Williams's phrase, "in the first draft," in the letter quoted above should not be taken to apply literally to the text of any play that appears in this edition. Certainly the designation cannot refer technically to our copy-texts for *Summer at the Lake, The Big Game,* or *The Fat Man's Wife*, all of which survive at HRC in earlier versions than those chosen for publication here.

During the early 1940s, while he completed full-length plays including *Battle of Angels, Stairs to The Roof,* and *You Touched Me!* (and, at length, *The Glass Menagerie* and *A Streetcar Named Desire),* Williams also continued to work on his one-acts. These included entries in *American Blues* series—which he had described in mid-1939 as "still in progress" (*Selected Letters* I, p. 180)—as well as texts that he filed mentally under other categories such as "Mississippi Sketches" and, mysteriously, "Dominos" (in a list from 1943; see Note to *Summer at the Lake*). In all this Williams was encouraged, surely, by the selection of several of his one-acts for performance and publication.

The exposure of Williams's shorter dramas to a public audience began in February, 1940, when *The Long Goodbye* was produced at The New School in New York City. Margaret Mayorga, editor of the annual anthology *Best One-Act Plays*, became one of Williams's important early champions by including his first published script (the short play *Moony's Kid Don't Cry*) in her 1940 volume, following it up with other one-act publications in succeeding years. In 1941, another one-act collection, *American Scenes*, edited by William Kozlenko, included two more plays by Williams.

According to unpublished correspondence filed in HRC (61.8), Kozlenko was negotiating in late 1940 for the rights to publish the four-play *American Blues* as a complete unit. However, pre-empted either by Mayorga's separate publication of *Moony's Kid Don't Cry*, or else by the agency's insistence on charging him the full publication rate for each individual play, Kozlenko settled instead for two different one-acts which he grouped under the title *Landscape With Figures* (*At Liberty* and *This Property Is Condemned*). Consequently, nothing ever became of *American Blues* as Williams had envisioned it since 1937. At length the title was demoted to a catch-all rubric for a pamphlet of five disparate short plays, published by the Dramatists Play Service in 1948 and still in print today. Throughout the later 1930s and earlier 1940s, however, Williams kept coming up with other groupings of one-acts that—like *American Blues* in any of its various incarnations—might be used to generate full dramatic programs.

During the latter half of 1941, when Williams probably typed the unfinished letter quoted at the beginning of this essay, he was casting about for new, potentially lucrative ideas and projects. He travelled to Provincetown, to the Gulf coast, to New York, to New Orleans, to his parents' home in Missouri, back to New

Orleans, and again to New York. At this time the nearest thing to a Prince Charming in his life was Hume Cronyn: a "rich actor" who, for "$50.00 a month," had purchased a option on Williams's one-acts (*Selected Letters* I, pp. 362, 328-9). That did not prevent Williams from looking to his short plays as possible sources of income from other places. In an unpublished letter to Audrey Wood dated October 28, 1941, filed at HRC (54.16), Williams enclosed an unidentified "short sketch" that, he said, was "removed from the long comedy... 'A Daughter of the American Revolution" (*i.e.,* part of what eventually became *The Glass Menagerie*). Williams predicted that the sketch "should serve to leaven any one-act program, if directed with sufficient legerdemain," and noted in a postscript: "New Theatre League offers $50.00 prize for a 15-minute skit – This <u>might</u> do – (the comedy)."

Of the scripts in *Mister Paradise and Other One-Act Plays*, at least one emerged from this difficult juncture in Williams's career. In an unpublished letter to Audrey Wood, written in New Orleans and dated October 27, 1941, Williams wrote, "I am enclosing two more one-acts which I have written in the past two days without barely reading them over. They might be combined [with] the sketch I sent you before in a group of three, called <u>Vieux Carré</u> and submitted to the Mayorga or Cronyn" (cf. *Selected Letters* I, p. 368). One of the three plays that Williams was now contemplating as candidates for Mayorga's or Cronyn's consideration was almost certainly *Thank You, Kind Spirit*.

Williams had mailed a draft of *Thank You, Kind Spirit* to Wood less than a week before writing to her on October 27. Moreover, we are able to identify two other one-acts that he set in the French Quarter during this time, and that were both published during the 1940s. Wood wrote to Williams in early November that a draft of *Lord Byron's Love Letter*, which she had recently received from him, seemed to contain "a commercial idea" (*Selected Letters* I, p. 358). Finally, in a journal entry from this period labeled "Monday Midnight," Williams stated: "I wrote a new one-act play today—'The Lady of Larkspur Lotion'—and feel not too badly" (Lyle Leverich, *Tom*, p. 432).

Mayorga shared Williams's good feeling about *The Lady of Larkspur Lotion*, which she selected for inclusion in *The Best One-Act Plays of 1941*. *Lord Byron's Love Letter* was published in 1945, in Williams's first collection of plays, *27 Wagons Full of Cotton and Other One-Acts* (also currently available in *Theatre VI*), along with *Hello From Bertha*, *The Long Good-bye*, *The Lady of Larkspur Lotion*, *This Property is Condemned*, and four other short plays. Now, with the publication of *Thank You, Kind Spirit*, it would possible to put on a program of three short plays entitled *Vieux Carré*, much as Williams must have envisioned it in the fall of 1941.

NOTES TO THE INDIVIDUAL PLAYS

The typed manuscripts of the first eleven plays in this volume are preserved in the Tennessee Williams Collection at the Harry Ransom Humanities Research Center, on the campus of the University of Texas at Austin. Of the copy-texts for the remaining two plays, one is in Michael Kahn's possession. The last is located in the Department of Special Collections at the University Research Library of the University of California, Los Angeles. In editing these manuscripts for a general readership, as well as for students and specialists, we have tried to convey what Williams wrote as directly and accurately as we can, subject to the reader's need for a clear and uncluttered presentation, and to the need of potential directors and actors for a workable performance text.

In three instances, we have had to choose between two or more complete drafts of a play in the archives, rejecting one or more extant alternative drafts. The principles of our selection in each case are different and may be found in the respective Notes.

In two other, exceptionally complex cases—also explained in the Notes—we have had to cut substantial portions of one script as Williams left it, while emending parts of the remainder for consistency (*And Tell Sad Stories of the Deaths of Queens . . .*), and have conflated two drafts of another play, each of which is missing some pages (*Adam and Eve on a Ferry*).

Our texts may not reflect particular changes, cuts, or alternative readings that have been preferred on occasion, whether by the directors of the stage productions listed earlier, or by directors of other staged readings and workshops.

All of our copy-texts were typed by Williams; many bear additional insertions, deletions, and comments written in Williams's hand. In some cases the intended location of an insertion, or the precise extent of a deletion, is partly subject to interpretation, yet in all of these instances we have been able to achieve a fair degree of confidence in our fidelity to Williams's text, and we do not note these cases individually.

Like all writers, Williams made occasional errors due to momentary lapses in memory or attention, as well as orthographical mistakes. Even his revised drafts look nothing like publishers' copy. They contain many incidental irregularities in format and presentation, not to mention obvious typing errors. We have emended a few inconsistent references in the dialogue to concrete details (such as names, places, periods of time and points in time), corrected what appear to be blatant misspellings, and, in many cases, normalized doubtful spellings. However, we have retained instances of the latter that may have been meant to reflect regionalisms, or to represent features of spoken dialect phonetically. Accidental typographical features, especially punctuation, have been subject to thoughtful editorial review and emendation.

Elements of dramatic texts that are conventionally presented in a thoroughly predictable format, such as speech headings and stage directions, have been regularized according to house-style. They have also been emended for consistency. This means that in most places where Williams's original stage directions lack articles or grammatical subjects, we have added them. In a few cases we have removed, added, or altered verbs related to particular actions in the stage directions (*e.g.*, replacing "crosses" with "walks.").

We have made the incidental and substantive emendations enumerated in the preceding two paragraphs silently. Our copy-texts for these plays are, in any event, available to the scrutiny of scholars and prospective directors, since they are held in publicly accessible archives (with the exception of the surviving draft of *The Municipal Abattoir*).

These are the Stairs You Got to Watch

Our copy-text is a unique typescript draft filed in HRC (49.7).

Since Carl refers to Joan Bennett as a "grandmother" (p. 5), the copy-text must have been drafted after Bennett's first grandchild was born in 1948 (by her own account).

A note in *Collected Stories* indicates that the story "The Mysteries of the Joy Rio" was written in New Orleans in 1941, although in a letter of November 22, 1946 he suggests that he got the idea for the story at that time: "I have an idea for a lovely long story about a sad little Mexican who repairs watches – called 'Joy Rio'" (*Selected Letters* II, p. 79). The Joy Rio then reappeared in another, derivative but different story entitled "Hard Candy."

Mister Paradise

Our copy-text is one of two typescript drafts filed in HRC (24.12).

Since the published version is set in the French Quarter, it seems almost certain that Williams wrote it in or after 1939, when he first visited New Orleans. An alternate version, in the same folder at HRC, is set in Greenwich Village and depicts the same action, but with substantially different dialogue. In early 1940, Williams's one-act play *The Long Good-bye* was performed in the Village, at the New School; in early 1942 he worked as a waiter in the same neighborhood. From this information, however, it is hard to deduce anything about the priority of either draft; Williams might well have chosen the Village as the setting for a script about a down-at-the-heels poet long before he ever saw it himself. To us, it appears that our copy-text is the later of the two scripts filed under this title. We have preferred the French Quarter version, in any case, because of what we judge to be its greater interest and superior quality. The Greenwich Village version, though possessing the advantage of fuller stage directions (see below), lacks the longer speeches which exist in our copy-text, and which approach the status of the "arias" for which Williams is famous in his more developed works.

Two handwritten draft versions of the play's final lines survive on a program for a series of film screenings held by the Museum of Modern Art Film Library, in Manhattan, which took place in October-November 1935; the program is now filed in HRC (53.2). These dialogue scraps are interesting, but as clues to the play's date they would seem useless, since it appears that Williams never set foot in New York between 1928 and 1939. Presumably the fragments were scribbled on the program years after it was printed, whenever and wherever Williams may have found it to hand.

In the New York version, Mr. Paradise is described as "a small middle-aged man" who opens the door "in crumpled purple pyjamas" worn under "a brown robe." His apartment is "an extremely squalid bedroom or 'studio' in Greenwich Village," with "a sky-light and slanting walls" and "utterly nondescript" furniture, including "a chiffonier with drawers hanging ajar, a marble-top wash-stand, a small iron bed in the alcove."

In our copy-text there is no opening stage direction. Based on the opening directions from the alternate version (quoted above) and on internal evidence from our copy-text, we have supplied a simple opening stage direction.

The Palooka

Our copy is a unique typescript draft filed in HRC (34.3).

In our Introduction to this volume we have discussed the range of dates that could be assigned to *The Palooka*. We cannot date the play with any degree of probability, except by making the plausible *a priori* assumption that Williams must have written it during the 1930s or 1940s.

Escape

Our copy-text is one of two extant typescript drafts, filed together in HRC (4.10).

Escape appears to be a product of the later 1930s or earlier 1940s, Williams's "apprentice" years. It would be pure speculation to assign a more particular date based on historical events, since the political reverberations of Scottsboro lasted from the 1930s through the 1960s and into the present. Williams must have been thinking about the case in other writings including a story from 1931-2, "Big Black: A Mississippi Idyll" (posthumously published in *Collected Stories);* a revised and unpublished version of that story, entitled "Bottle of Brass" (see below); and an unpublished longer one-act play (probably from the late 1930 or early 1940s) entitled *Jungle,* at HRC (22.2). He would allude to lynching and related issues again in his full-length play of 1940, *Battle of Angels,* and its later successors, *Orpheus Descending* and the film *Fugitive Kind.* An untitled short script filed in HRC (53.6) features two men in jail, Bum and Lem, who, though not Black themselves, discuss the fate of lynched Black men.

One of the two drafts of *Escape* in HRC bears an alternate title, "Bottle of Brass," which Williams cancelled, but which appears elsewhere as the title of drafts for an unpublished short story filed in HRC (4.10) and among the unsorted drafts in Box 53. The story, "Bottle of Brass," is a revised and expanded version of the posthumously published early work "Big Black: A Mississippi Idyll" (in *Collected Stories).* The phrase "Bottle of Brass" refers to a bottled spirit in the *Arabian Nights,* according to an epigraph in Williams's unpublished story. Both the published and unpublished versions of the story, in any case, are entirely different from the present one-act—except in so far as all depict African American men on the run from racist whites.

Why Do You Smoke So Much, Lily?

Our copy-text is a unique typescript filed in HRC (51.16), at the end of which Williams has hand-written "Feb. 1935." The script is filed along with a short story, which bears the same title, and contains virtually the same action and dialogue.

An alternate version of Lily's attempt to cope with her situation occurs in the unpublished, less focused playlet *Lily and La Vie,* or *The Chain Cigarette,* filed in HRC (23.10), where Lily's problem is focused more simply on sexual frustration. After discussing her dissatisfaction with an effeminate male literary friend, Lily ends the play by running out the door after a virile delivery boy named Butch. The conclusion suggests a distant kinship between Lily Yorke and Blanche DuBois, whose libido is aroused by the young subscription-collector in *A Streetcar Named Desire,* as well as Lily's relationship to Alma Winemiller in *Summer and Smoke* and *The Eccentricities of a Nightingale.*

Summer at the Lake

Our copy-text is one of three complete typescript drafts, filed along with fragments of at least one later, but incomplete draft in HRC (12.10 and 47.1). Some of these materials are filed under the alternate title "Escape," though none are related to the other, very different one-act play which is published in this volume as *Escape* (cf. our Note above to that play). "Escape" is also the title under which *Summer at the Lake* was produced in 2004 as part of *Five By Tenn.* We have preferred the title *Summer at the Lake,* in part because it was Williams's latest title for a draft of this play, and in part to distinguish it from the other play here titled *Escape.*

Our copy-text must have been composed before 1939, since it bears the name "Thomas Lanier Williams" on its title-page; it is evidently the second, rather than the third of the three complete drafts in order of composition. An apparently later draft is preserved in the file, also bearing the name "Thomas Lanier Williams" (and therefore predating 1939); it incorporates some of Williams's handwritten additions on our copy-text, and also introduces further changes to the dialogue, both typewritten and handwritten. However, the file at HRC contains other typescript fragments that must have originated still later than either of these complete versions. Clearly, throughout the later 1930s and the early 1940s, the materials for *Summer at the Lake* were undergoing a continual process of evolution; ultimately they were subsumed by a vastly dissimilar, unfinished project (see below).

We have preferred our copy-text, first, because it has a more complete appearance, including a detailed opening stage-direction (which its successor draft lacks). Secondly, we prefer our copy-text because in most respects it is dramatically superior to the draft that followed it, at least in our judgment—a judgment that accords with Michael Kahn's selection of our copy-text as the version to be premiered in *Five By Tenn*.

What appears to be the earliest complete, extant draft of *Summer at the Lake* lacks speech headings, has few stage directions, and bears two alternative titles in Williams's handwriting ("The Lake" and "Quicksilver"). Our copy-text—which, as stated, was probably the penultimate rather than the latest of the three complete drafts—bears the title "Escape," handwritten above two other cancelled alternate titles ("Quicksilver" and "The Lake," both typewritten). The third, and probably the latest complete draft bears the title "Summer At The Lake," handwritten above the alternate typed title "Escape" (which has not been cancelled). On the title-page of this third complete draft, Williams wrote the annotation "American Blues: III" and designated the script as a "First draft."

Williams's use of his given name on what appears to be the latest complete draft of *Summer at the Lake* shows that all the extant, complete versions were done before the beginning of 1939. Among the related fragments in the files at HRC, however, there is another typed title-page for *Summer at the Lake* on which Williams gave the name "Tennessee Williams." This shows both that Williams finally settled on "Summer At The Lake" as the play's title, and also that he continued revising the play, or at least intended to revise it, in or after 1939. Indeed, a fragmentary draft of dialogue from the play exists in HRC (53.3), written on stationery from the YMCA in New York City (356 West 34th St.), where Williams stayed in the first half of 1940, again during the "late spring" of 1941 (*Selected Letters* I, p. 317), and yet again in March, 1943. The title "Summer at the Lake" also appears on a two-page typed list, evidently from 1943, in which Williams identified the names and locations of his currently circulating "properties" or manuscripts; this list is now filed in HRC (54.16) together with two letters that Williams wrote to Audrey Wood in May, 1943.

Some time between the end of 1937 and mid-1940 (most likely in 1939) Williams drafted a scenario, now filed in HRC (47.1), for another, longer play entitled "Summer at the Lake" or "Words are a Net to Catch Beauty." The phrase "Nets to catch beauty" appears in related dialogue fragments in HRC (53.6) in which a youth drowns himself by swimming out too far, but—very unlike Donald Fenway—leaves behind a cache of literary manuscripts. Williams seems to have been recurrently preoccupied with the image of the young man disappearing into the water, experimenting with different contexts for this event, and imagining various possible motives for such an action.

In the handwritten fragment on YMCA stationery, after the play's last line of dialogue ("He didn't come back"), Williams wrote a closing stage direction that does not appear on the other drafts: "The gulls are heard crying outside as they circle close to the windows." A seagull is also mentioned, albeit less prominently, in our copy-text, along with various incidental echoes of Chekhov, whose work Williams discovered in the 1930s and the playwright who had the greatest influence on Williams. In the 1970s and 1980s Williams adapted Chekov's play, *The Seagull*, under his own title, *The Notebook of Trigorin*.

The Big Game

Our copy-text is one of two typescript drafts, filed in HRC (4.3), which Williams probably prepared in 1937.

At the end of our copy-text, Williams wrote his name (as "T. L. Williams") above the street address, "6634 Pershing." Between

September, 1935 and July, 1937, the Williams family resided at this location in Saint Louis. Also, in a fragmentary draft of a dialogue between two characters named "Pierrot" and "Pierrette" (HRC 53.3), one page was typed on the reverse of a typed title-page for "THE BIG GAME (A one-act play)." Since it was in 1937 that Williams submitted a play entitled "The Death of Pierrot" to a local play contest (Leverich 211), it would seem most likely that he was at work on *The Big Game* during this year. (In this rogue title-page, the "Time" is specified as "Autumn of the present year, A Saturday.")

In the alternate draft, which was evidently earlier, Williams's opening stage direction suggests that Tony should have a more obviously stereotypical appearance. "He is evidently the recipient of all kinds of attention and he's the type of boy that deserves it, fresh, hearty, exuberant, magnificently normal." The other boy, the "Dave" of our copy-text (in the alternate draft he remains nameless), "is evidently less fortunate. On his table is a single vase of withered flowers of the inexpensive kind."

The Pink Bedroom

Our copy-text, a unique typed draft, is filed in HRC (35.4).

Presumably this playlet was completed by May, 1943, since the title appears on the two-page typed list of Williams's "properties" (described earlier, in the Note to *Summer at the Lake).* In fact, the title "The Pink Bedroom" appears twice on that 1943 list: once as the title of a short play, and again as the title of a short story.

Twelve years earlier, in 1931, Williams had submitted a short story entitled "The Pink Bedroom" to a student fiction contest at the University of Missouri, according to recently published research (Philip C. Kolin, "'No masterpiece has been overlooked': The Early Reception and Significance of Tennessee Williams's 'Big Black: A Mississippi Idyll,'" *ANQ*, Vol. 8, No. 4, pp. 27-34). A story by Williams entitled "The Pink Bedroom" survives in HRC, where it is filed along with the play. Its plot, though, is substantially different.

The image of the pink bedroom, and an odd response to pink as a peculiarly disconcerting color, appear elsewhere in Williams's writing. In typescript fragments that are currently filed among Williams's untitled or unsorted materials in HRC (Box 53), a European writer-director turned Hollywood screenwriter provides his "modern Galatea" with an entirely pink bedroom. And, in the early play *Stairs to the Roof*, a character is told by her employer that "I'd rather you didn't wear pink – I have an allergy to it" (*Stairs to the Roof* [New York: New Directions, 2000], p. 18).

The Fat Man's Wife

Our copy-text is a typescript, filed in HRC (13.1).

Below the title on the copy-text, Williams gives his name as "Thomas Lanier Williams," meaning that this draft was completed in or before 1939. In the copy-text, the play is set on New Year's morning in 1938. However, alternate drafts in HRC, filed with this one, set the action on New Year's morning, 1937. It may be concluded plausibly that Williams wrote some versions of the play in 1937, and then completed the text as published here in 1938 (or, perhaps, when 1938 was approaching).

An alternate draft bears the annotation "First draft" in Williams's handwriting. An alternate title, "The Chance Acquaintance," appears among the drafts in HRC.

An undated page of Williams's reflections in HRC (53.3) shows that at some point—possibly for a formal course in the drama—he read Bernard Shaw's play, *Candida,* the theme of which resembles that of *The Fat Man's Wife* (see Introduction). The fragment expresses Williams's puzzlement at Shaw's moral, perhaps explaining part of the reason why Williams attempted to dramatize a similar scenario.

Thank You, Kind Spirit

Our copy-text is a unique typescript draft filed in HRC (49.4).

In a letter to Audrey Wood dated October 21, 1941, Williams indicated clearly that he had written this play shortly before he wrote the letter: "In response to the request for another one-act I have hastily banged out this little sketch of a spiritualist meeting I attended here in the quarter a few nights ago. – It did not end so dramatically as here represented but the characters are from life" (*Selected Letters* I, p. 350). In an undated journal entry from the same period, Williams wrote: "Visited a chapel – spiritualist earlier in the evening. In the A.M. wrote a new scene in play and a short story." And, in a somewhat later entry which is simply dated "Tuesday," Williams reported with satisfaction: "Good humor returned with the sale of a suit, good food, the writing and dispatching of a 1-act about the spiritualist, and a kind letter from Audrey." Both journal entries survive in the same notebook, filed in HRC (21.15).

In HRC (54.16) there is another, unpublished letter from Williams to Wood, dated October 27, 1941, that illustrates his intentions for three plays to be grouped together under the collective title *Vieux Carré*. The proximity in the dates makes it all but certain that this "group of three" included *Thank You, Kind Spirit* (see discussion above, at the beginning of the Notes).

The Municipal Abattoir

Our copy-text—the only text of this play that we know to be extant—is currently in the possession of Michael Kahn, Artistic Director of the Shakespeare Theatre in Washington, D.C. Kahn received the script from Lee Hoiby, to whom Williams gave the play after Hoiby worked on the operatic version of *Summer and Smoke*.

Williams seems to have been revising *The Municipal Abattoir* in 1966, when this title was included—along with that of *The Two-Character Play*—on a list of titles for possible inclusion in the volume *Dragon Country and Other Plays*. (Both entries were then crossed out, with a notation: "TW still working on.") The list, written in Williams's hand and dated March 11, 1966, survives in the files at New Directions.

The Municipal Abattoir has some thematic links to a short story of 1937 entitled "The Treadmill," which was published posthumously in an edition by Allean Hale, as well as to the poem "The Death Embrace" and other writings about impersonal and oppressive governments such as *Camino Real.*

Adam and Eve on a Ferry

We produced the present, edited text by conflating portions of two substantially complete, yet partly defective typescripts filed in HRC (1.4).

Williams must have written this play after July 1939, since it features the ferry between Oakland and San Francisco on which he traveled that month, during his first visit to the Bay area.

We made the editorial decision to combine parts of two different drafts because both of the surviving scripts are marred by significant lacunae. Whereas one draft (A) lacks one or more pages in the middle, the other draft (B) has a middle, but lacks one or more pages at the beginning and one or more pages at the end. Moreover, a separate page contains an alternate, apparently revised version of the original ending to to A; we have followed this revision (see below).

In our view, the essential similarity between the two scripts justifies their interpretation as variant texts of a single work. While it is difficult to be certain which draft was chronologically prior, both appear to have been produced at around the same time.

So that our procedure may be as transparent as possible to the reader, we here present the following guide to our conflated text.

From the opening stage direction through Lawrence's line, "Don't bring that thing in here!" we follow A.

From the Visitor's reply ("Oh, I beg your—!") through Lawrence's line, "Whispered *what?*" we follow B.

From the Visitor's reply ("He whispered his name . . .") through the Visitor's line, "He also mentioned the name of a certain hotel," we follow A.

From Lawrence's reply ("And you did what?") through Lawrence's line, "Luckily you had been left some money in trust by an Aunt?" we follow B (restoring the word "Aunt," cancelled in the copy-text).

From the Visitor's reply ("Not an Aunt—an Uncle.") through the Visitor's line, "O'Reilly, O'Reilly, Adam O'Reilly!" and the subsequent direction, we follow A (with "Adam" substituted here for the copy-text's "Clarence").

Finally, from the Visitor's line, "Oh, Mr. Lawrence, now, now, now I remember!" through the end of the present edition, we follow a one-page typescript that appears to be Williams' last revision of the conclusion to A (unlike B, it shares A's unusually wide left typewriter margin, and the change of name from "Clarence" to "Adam" evidently represents an afterthought whereby Williams added to the play's symbolism).

This completes our account of the relation between the present edition of *Adam and Eve on a Ferry* and the manuscripts at HRC. However, we may also note the presence in the file at HRC (1.4) of a lone page, perhaps representing an intermediate stage of the play (between A and B), that depicts a fascinatingly different conclusion to the encounter. It begins as Lawrence "GOES ABOUT KICKING OVER THE POTTED PLANTS," apparently enraged in some way related to the presence of these tokens sent by his "friends and admirers." Lawrence then announces, "This concludes the audience, Miss Preston." The Visitor wrings her hands and replies, "Oh, but Mr. Lawrence – I hoped – hoped – hoped – !" Lawrence retorts, "Yes, I know what you hoped[.] You hoped that I with a word could undo centuries of wrong-thinking, all of the mischief committed by stupid, sterile intellectualism pointing the finger of shame at the sensible flesh. Unfortunately I can't do that, Miss Preston. There's a new clean wind that's going to blow through the world and it's going to blow all the dry old dust off the furniture of the world. But that takes time, dear lady. – Me, I've only kicked up a breeze, a very little breeze! The great big death-giving and <u>life-beginning</u> tornado – comes after my time." At last he advises the Visitor, "Your only possible course of action is plain. You will have to go back, and retrace your footsteps to Adam." When the Visitor ("wonderingly") responds, "Adam?" then Lawrence continues, "Yes, Adam, Adam, the everlasting Adam! The one who embraced you – openly – On a San Francisco ferry!" To which the Visitor, reacting "with sudden conviction, the dawn of a new world," replies: "Adam! – ADAM! That was his name, it was Adam, Adam O'Reilly!" The rest of this alternate draft is cut short by the end of the sole surviving page in the file.

A few further notes are needed here with regard to the discussion of this play in our Introduction. First, as Annette Saddik has reminded us, the phrase "One of those rare electrical things between people" adumbrates a phrase spoken by Blanche Dubois in *A Streetcar Named Desire* (with reference to the meeting of Stanley and Stella): "Now don't say it was one of those mysterious electric things between people! If you do I'll laugh in your face" (*Theatre* I, p. 320). If the image originated in the context of *Adam and Eve on a Ferry,* then its original association with Lawrence's teachings on sexuality may shed light on Blanche's complex feelings. Second, Williams's prefatory remarks on the first complete draft of *You Touched Me!,* which we quoted in the Introduction, survive in HRC (53.1). Finally, Williams's reference to Lawrence as "a funny little man" is quoted from published correspondence of late 1941 (*Selected Letters* I, 346).

And Tell Sad Stories of the Deaths of Queens . . .

Our copy-text is a draft at UCLA (University Research Library, Special Collections, Tennessee Williams, box 1, folder 2).

Accompanying Williams's manuscripts at UCLA is a letter dated September 9, 1970, in which Williams attested to his authorship of the texts preserved there, with annotations on each item in the collection. Williams's note for *And Tell Sad Stories of the Deaths of Queens...* reads as follows: "A play in two scenes. Complete, unproduced, unpublished. A tragi-comedy concerning a transvestite's adoration for a rough merchant-seaman in the Vieux Carré of New Orleans. Written in Havana shortly before Castro regime: also lost and recovered in Miami storage house. About 31 pages, a rough first draft, in author's typing with author's hand-written corrections, Etc. – Requires revisions: production rights reserved by author." This information should not be assumed to be accurate in every detail (for instance, the draft is indeed "rough" but contains portions of second or subsequent drafts). Based on the note, however, we can probably date the beginning of Williams's work on this play to 1957, a year when he visited Havana and stayed in the Comodoro—the name that appears on the hotel stationery on which he typed part of the extant script. (For corroborating evidence of his stay at the Comodoro cf. *Tennessee Williams's Letters to Donald Windham* [New York, 1977], p. 293.) Other pages in the surviving draft are typed on stationery from "The Colony Hotel, Palm Beach, Florida" and "The Robert Clay, Miami." When Candy alludes to "the war-years" as though they are now at least seventeen years in the past (p. 191), we may infer tentatively that Williams was still working on the play at some point between 1958 and 1962.

To sum up our case for the date of *And Tell Sad Stories of the Deaths of Queens . . .* , it appears that while the initial concept for the play may have occurred to Williams in 1957, he must have returned to it within the next five years. It may well have been as late as 1970 when he finally put together a complete script from all his drafts.

Williams used different typewriters for different parts of this script. In fact, there is abundant internal evidence—including inconsistencies in the names of characters and redundancies in the dramatic action—showing that Williams combined parts of at least two, substantially different drafts of this play in order to produce the text that was deposited in the archive. (For instance, in what appear to be the earliest portions of the composite text, the character ultimately called "Karl" was named "Buck.") As a result, this play poses an unusual editorial challenge. To eliminate Williams's inadvertent redundancies, in order to produce a readable and performable text, we have made more substantial changes here than in the other edited texts that comprise this volume.

On p. **189**, the first sentence in the opening stage direction is non-authorial and has been added.

On p. **193** we have added a non-authorial stage direction, "*Turns his attention to the photo again.*"

On p. **196**, we have adapted the direction beginning "*During this or his next long speech . . .*" from a retrospective direction originally placed by Williams after Candy's long speech, on p. 197.

On p. **206** we have added a non-authorial stage direction, "*She pours bourbon and goes out to the garden,*" and have inserted the non-authorial words, "*A splash is heard, followed by*" and "*As the lights come back up,*" into Williams's next stage direction.

On pp. **208** and **209-210**, we have cut many lines that, in the copy-text, relate to an alternate, second version of Candy's prior phone-call to the stripper. Evidently, Williams overlooked the redundancy of this conversation here, and left it in by mistake. However, we have preserved Karl's question, "When did she say she'd get here?" (which, in the copy-text, refers to the redundant phone-call that is here omitted). Finally, we have emended the rest of the scene slightly to make it consistent with the information provided earlier (p. **204**)—replacing three brief lines in the copy-text with Candy's single line, "Nine-thirty" (changed from Williams's "nine"), and replacing Karl's "five of nine" in the copy-text with "nine." The closing stage direction in Scene One is non-authorial and has been added.

On p. **211**, at the beginning of Scene Two, we have constructed the stage direction that appears in our edition by restoring portions of a cancelled direction in the copy-text, and condensing these together with the cursory, handwritten direction with which Williams replaced it—"(A week later) Sunday A.M., rain." Williams apparently cancelled the earlier, longer direction because it no longer served, as it once had, as an opening direction for the beginning of a new play. (The original, cancelled stage direction here reads: "A rainy winter morning in New Orleans. A queen on her thirty-fifth birthday is having coffee and Knox gelatine in fruit juice at a daintily set breakfast-table on which is a pale blue Japanese vase of pussy-willows. The entire room is decorated in a Japanese fashion. The queen is unhappy on this birthday morn, feeling her youth has gone by. In the next room of her two-room apartment, someone is sleeping loudly. All of her motions and actions are muted not to disturb the loud sleeper. Presently another, younger queen enters without knocking. This one is still under thirty, is handsome but with a pinched look and a humorous lisp.")

In two instances on p. **213**, following Karl's requests for "vodka" and "ice-cubes," we have substituted two specific stage directions where Williams wrote simply, "Same business."

On pp. **216**, **217**, and **218**, we have substituted the name "Alice Jackson" for a different name ("Clare Hackett") that appears in the copy-text. This is part of our policy of regularizing character names throughout the play, though here the change is also motivated by a clear dramatic advantage.

The song, "Poor Butterfly" (p. **189**), is presumably the popular tune by Golden and Hubbell (1916). For the poem recited by Candy (p. **199**), see *The Collected Poems of Tennessee Williams,* ed. David Roessel and Nicholas Moschovakis (New York: New Directions, 2002), pp. **150**, **254**.

Filed in HRC (24.12), as well as among the unsorted scripts in Box 53, are drafts of a related playlet, in some cases entitled "The Meeting of People." Among these drafts are pages typed on Havana hotel stationery. Some passages closely resemble parts of the present text, and the conception as a whole is strikingly similar. In the untitled version from Box 53, set in "A bedroom in a lower second class hotel in New Orleans," a woman named Mrs. Venable confronts a younger sailor named "Jim Casky," who has woken up in her bed with a severe hangover and takes it into his head to believe that that he has been robbed; near the end of this draft, Mrs. Venable tells Casky ironically: "I supplied the money and you the charm." At one point in the same draft, when reports arrive that the hotel management is outraged at Mrs. Venable's having a male guest who is not registered with her, she proposes telling them that she is "flying tomorrow to Havana."

"Venable," of course, is a name that Williams used for characters in his longer play, *Suddenly Last Summer*. Intriguingly, the title "And Tell Sad Stories of the Deaths of Queens" also appears among early materials for *Suddenly Last Summer* at HRC (Boxes 14 and 15).

ABBREVIATIONS OF SOURCES CITED
IN THE NOTES

Collected Stories	Tennessee Williams, *Collected Stories* (New York: New Directions, 1985)
HRC	Harry Ransom Humanities Research Center, Tennessee Williams Collection. (The first and second numbers enclosed in parentheses following "HRC" designate, respectively, the numbers of the box and of the folder in which the materials cited are currently filed.)
Leverich	Lyle Leverich, *Tom: The Unknown Tennessee Williams* (New York: Crown, 1995)
Selected Letters I	*The Selected Letters of Tennessee Williams,* Volume I (1920–1945), ed. Albert J. Devlin and Nancy M. Tischler (New York: New Directions, 2000)
Selected Letters II	*The Selected Letters of Tennessee Williams,* Volume II (1945–1957), ed. Albert J. Devlin, co-ed. Nancy M. Tischler (New York: New Directions, 2004)
Theatre	*The Theatre of Tennessee Williams, Volumes I through VIII.* (New York: New Directions, 1971-1992)

New Directions Paperbooks—A Partial Listing

For a complete listing request a free catalog from New Directions, 80 Eighth Avenue, New York, NY 10011; or visit our website, www.ndpublishing.com

†Bilingua

For a complete listing request a free catalog from New Directions, 80 Eighth Avenue
New York, NY 10011; or visit our website, www.ndpublishing.com

†Bilingual

ONE-ACT PLAY COLLECTIONS
by TENNESSEE WILLIAMS

27 WAGONS FULL OF COTTON
Thirteen one-act plays

27 Wagons Full of Cotton ✦ The Purification ✦ The Lady of Larkspur Lotion
The Last of My Solid Gold Watches ✦ Portrait of a Madonna ✦ Auto-Da-Fé
Lord Byron's Love Letter ✦ The Strangest Kind of Romance
The Long Goodbye ✦ Hello From Bertha ✦ This Property is Condemned
Something Unspoken ✦ The Unsatisfactory Supper
Talk to Me Like the Rain and Let Me Listen

MISTER PARADISE
AND OTHER ONE-ACT PLAYS

Edited, with an introduction, by Nicholas Moschovakis and David Roessel
Foreword by Eli Wallach and Anne Jackson

These Are the Stairs You Got to Watch ✦ Mister Paradise
The Palooka ✦ Escape ✦ Why Do You Smoke So Much, Lily?
Summer At The Lake ✦ The Big Game ✦ The Pink Bedroom
The Fat Man's Wife ✦ Thank You, Kind Spirit
The Municipal Abattoir ✦ Adam and Eve on a Ferry
And Tell Sad Stories of The Deaths of Queens...

THE TRAVELING COMPANION
AND OTHER PLAYS

Edited, with an introduction, by Annette Saddik

The Chalky White Substance ✦ The Day on Which a Man Dies
A Cavalier for Milady ✦ The Pronoun 'I'
The Remarkable Rooming-House of Madame LeMonde
Kirche, Küche, Kinder ✦ Green Eyes ✦ The Parade
The One Exception ✦ Sunburst
Will Mr. Merriwether Return from Memphis? (full-length)
The Traveling Companion

DRAGON COUNTRY
A book of nine short plays

In the Bar   3 1901 04368 2071   e Phoenix
The Mu............   ....ssional
The Frosted Glass Coffin ✦ The Gnädiges Fräulein
A Perfect Analysis Given by a Parrot